Colton

Cerberus Mc Book 14
Marie James

Copyright

Colton: Cerberus MC Book 14
Copyright © 2020 Marie James
Editing by Marie James Betas & Ms. K Edits
EBooks are not transferrable. All rights are reserved. No part of this book may be used or reproduced in any manner without written permission, except in the case of brief quotations embodied in critical articles and reviews. The unauthorized reproduction or distribution of this copyrighted work is illegal. No part of this book may be scanned, uploaded, or distributed via the Internet or any other means, electronic or print, without the publisher's permission.

This book is a work of fiction. The names, characters, places, and incidents are products of the writer's imagination or have been used fictitiously and are not to be construed as real. Any resemblance to persons, living or dead, actual events, locale, or organizations is entirely coincidental.

Acknowledgements

I still can't believe this is my life!

Years ago if anyone ever told me I'd be able to write stories and people would read them, I would've called them a liar, but here I am living the dream!

These dreams didn't happen by my efforts alone. It takes an entire village, and most days the villagers are the ones running the show and keeping me in line!

First let me say a little shout out to my husband, who does his best to keep me motivated and works very hard to create a calm working environment so I can get the stories down. Love you, babe!

Secondly, Christine Estevez (Wildfire PR) I couldn't do this without you. Like for real. Left to my own devices, I'd lay in bed all day and eat Cheetos. Thank you for your continued support. It means everything to me!

Laura Watson! You girl are absolute FIRE! You're my right and left hands, and I'd flop around like a crazed person if you weren't around to help me out!

Mary (Ms. K Edits) you take what I have and make it better, and not only am I so grateful, I'm sure the readers are happy they don't get a jumbled mess! Thank you!

BETA girls! (MaRanda, Laura, Michelle, Brenda, Jo) You ladies amaze me with your keen eyes and attention to detail! Thank you SO much for helping me out!

Wildfire PR and RRR Promotions, thank you for your time in helping get this book in reader's hands!

ARC Team! You guys are phenomenal! You hype me up like a champion, and for that I can't thank you enough! It keeps me motivated and inspires me to keep going!

Readers, without you, none of this would be possible. Thank you for your years of support!

~ Marie James

Synopsis

Detective Colton Matthews has experienced a lot in the last ten years.
Promotions.
Divorce.
Single-dad life.
His work life is as full of surprises as his home life.
But nothing prepared him for *her*.
Saying yes to the favor asked of the Cerberus MC was a no-brainer.
He's a good guy, helping other good guys.
How hard would it be to allow Sophia, Dominic Anderson's daughter, to shadow him for a few months to complete a college credit and keep things professional?
The short answer...
Impossible.
Especially when his job puts her in danger.

Chapter 1

Colton

"That's correct," I sigh, head bent over my keyboard, eyes squeezed shut as if it will help to stave off the irritation of having to deal with this for a third time. "I submitted my request two weeks ago."

"We can't find it, Detective Matthews. You'll have to submit it again." The voice on the other end of the line seems just as annoyed as I'm feeling.

Mondays suck.

Pinching the bridge of my nose, I take another deep breath. The first ten didn't help, and this one doesn't seem like it's going to either.

"That's the same thing I was told last week, so I submitted the request again. Is there a supervisor I can speak with?"

"Hold, please."

Ridiculous elevator music fills the line as my eyes dart to the growing stack of cases on my desk. Farmington isn't a huge town, so every questionable death lands in front of me. I contemplate taking a vacation, but I know the work will only be waiting for me when I return.

"Hey."

My eyes snap up to the doorway. I've only been at work for twenty minutes, but I'm still not capable of reflecting back the grin that's being aimed at me.

I raise an eyebrow when my chief doesn't immediately open his mouth to speak.

"What's up?"

"Don't forget you have Professor Wesley from that community college coming today."

How could I forget?

The answer is simple, I have a million other things to worry about than entertaining the idea of speaking to a bunch of gore-hungry college students about police work. They don't want to know a damn thing about the ins and outs of the job. Of course their questions start off simple, but they always end with wanting to know about the gruesome side of the job. I blame television for desensitizing today's youth.

"Tell me that isn't today."

"It is," Chief Monahan confirms as he looks down at his watch. "She should be here any minute."

"Thanks," I mumble, holding up a finger when the music stops and someone comes back on the line.

"Detective Matthews?"

"Still here," I mutter because her voice is filled with the hopefulness that I've hung up the phone while waiting.

"I've found your request for those documents. I'll start processing it now."

"Will it be expedited due to the delay?"

Light from the outer room fills my office when Monahan walks away.

"Did the precinct pay for the rush fee?" My eyes narrow.

"No, but the initial request was made over two weeks ago."

"Without the correct fees applied, it will be five business days."

"Perfect." It's anything but perfect, but the request is for a cold case I've been dabbling with for the last six months. Another week, honestly, won't make a difference.

"The requested documents will be ready for pickup next Monday."

My lip twitches, the agitation I've felt since my alarm went off this morning coming to a head.

"Thank you," I tell the clerk before dropping the phone back on the receiver.

If my first thirty minutes at work is a reflection of how today is going to go, I may need that vacation after all. With my eyes closed, I roll my head around on my shoulders, but the back-and-forth motion doesn't alleviate the stress that's been building nonstop since I graduated from the academy fourteen years ago.

"Looks like you could use a massage."

My eyes snap open, but before I can open my mouth to tell the interloper to fuck off, I notice her smile.

Yes, it's the first thing I see, but I'm a cop, so the ability to take in the full picture in the blink of an eye is a skill I honed many, many years ago.

Mysterious dark eyes, haloed by long lashes, watch me. A slender neck leads to a regretfully fully buttoned blouse. The no doubt sexy curve of her breasts is hidden behind a suit jacket. The soft flare of her hips is covered by a pencil skirt that flirts at the top of her knees. Her tan skin glistens, which should be an anomaly considering the harsh florescent lights.

She's utter perfection. Younger than I would think a college professor would be, but what the hell do I know? There's so much cosmetic stuff on the market these days, fifty is the new thirty-five. Going by that math, I'd say this woman may look no older than twenty-five, but she's probably about ten years older—same age as me.

Suddenly, helping this woman out with her class seems like the best idea my chief has ever tossed my way. When her smile widens, I understand completely. As a married man, Monahan probably didn't want the trouble that would come with this woman. Not that he would cheat, the man is as loyal as they come, but this woman is clearly meant for sin.

"May I have a seat?"

I blink up at her, my brain refusing to come back online.

"What?"

"A seat?" She points a perfectly manicured nail at the chair in front of my desk.

"Oh, yeah." I stand like a starstruck idiot and point.

She chuckles, and it makes me wonder if she gets this reaction all the time. I wouldn't doubt it. I see crazy stuff nearly every day, and I'm certain this is the first time my brain has been fried by a good-looking woman.

"Monahan reminded me this morning you'd be here."

Her brow furrows, and I give myself an internal pat on the back. It's the only way I can think to regain some power, to let her know I may be acting like a fool now, but that I haven't been waiting around for her to show up.

"Who?"

"Chief Monahan," I clarify.

She gives me a small smile as she lowers a leather computer bag beside the chair at her feet.

"I'll be honest, I don't know Chief Monahan very well. I think I've only met him once."

"Great guy," I say as I settle back in my chair. "Surprised you wanted to meet with me instead of him."

"I'm not very interested in the administrative side of the department, Detective Matthews."

Is her voice actually as sultry as it sounds when she says my name, or has it just been too long since I've had a woman under me?

I clear my throat, the office being no place to even contemplate the things that seem to want to infiltrate my head right now.

"What exactly are you interested in?"

I lean back in my office chair, finding it strange that I'm being weird about where my hands are situated. Clasping them together, I settle them on my lap, but then realize I look like a teen trying to hide an erection, so I curl my fingers around the armrests. The woman is smoking hot, but I'm a grown-ass man in control of my damn body.

Then she shifts, lifting her leg slightly to cross it over her other, and my hands go right back to my lap.

Clearing my throat, I scoot further under my desk.

"You seem a little out of sorts." She bends, the top buttons on her blouse stretching and sadly holding when she reaches into her laptop bag. "Is it because it's Monday or does every day on the job stress you out?"

My brain doesn't come back online again until she straightens in her chair with a notebook on her lap and a pen in her hand.

"Some days are better than others."

"You make it sound like all days have some degree of bad."

"I'm a homicide detective," I remind her. "Every day is bad for someone."

Her smile drops from her pretty face when she takes in the gravity of my words.

"You don't seem as rabid for information. Are the students in your class the same?"

I'm probably not the first person she's approached to speak to her class. Most criminal justice programs are smaller, and the students take the majority of the classes offered. I imagine recycling the same guest speakers would get boring.

"I guess like with any class, the personalities range from disinterested to rabid as you called it." She lifts the end of her pen to her mouth, her plump lips pursing against it, and I'm fascinated at the sight.

I can't concentrate, not even a little.

"I have a pretty full schedule today. Maybe we should get together over dinner to discuss the finer details?" I keep my focus on her mouth, praying she's savvy enough to understand my hesitation to continue a discussion in my office.

"Dinner?" My skin heats when her gaze focuses on my own mouth. "It's not even nine yet. We could get so much done between now and then."

"We could," I agree. "But I have to work."

"Won't you be tired by the end of your shift?"

"I have a very good feeling my energy level won't be an issue."

"No?" That fucking pen teases her lower lip, and the erection I was certain I could keep at bay is throbbing behind the zipper of my slacks.

I lower my voice. "Not a chance. We could meet at Wright's, the little diner off Main. Say six o'clock?"

"For dinner?"

"Yes."

"Seems like a waste of time." Her eyes lift to mine, sparkling with mischief and desire. "Wouldn't the Hampton Inn be better?"

"Get right to the point?" I tease.

"Is there any other way?"

"We'll have to discuss your class, eventually."

"It can wait another day, or we could chat while you're recharging."

"You assume you'll wear me out."

"I know I will." Perfect teeth dig into her lower lip, and although I've never done it before, I have the sudden urge to feign illness and leave for the day.

I shift in my seat, and she gives me a knowing look.

"Besides," she leans closer, "are you really going to get anything done with a hard co—"

"Matthews!"

Guiltily, I snap my head up, and I want to unleash a territorial growl when Detective Haden Gaffey smiles down at my visitor.

"What?" I snap, but he ignores me.

"Are you serious?" Gaffey asks the woman opposite of me as he draws closer. "I didn't know I'd be seeing your beautiful face today."

"Haden," the professor says with an easy smile.

I nearly come unglued like a psycho when she stands and his arms automatically go around her waist.

"You look amazing. How's your dad?"

"He's good. Staying busy with work. You know how it is."

I release a breath I didn't know I was holding when she steps back, putting a couple feet of distance between them.

Gaffey has been on the police force for almost twenty years, and he was one of my training officers when I was first hired. I've always respected the hell out of the man, and it's shocking I was ready to chew his face off when he first walked in here.

"Don't let this one give you a hard time," Gaffey says, hitching his thumb over his shoulder in my direction.

Oh, I have a hard time for her alright.

She grins at me. "I can handle him."

"Yeah?" Gaffey laughs. "I don't imagine it'll be too bad working with him. I don't think there's a man alive that would want to get on the wrong side of your dad."

She rolls her eyes, making her appear much younger than her attire is hinting at.

"It's good to see you, Soph." Gaffey turns in my direction. "That professor from the college is waiting in the lobby for you."

He walks away, but my eyes snap to the woman in front of me.

Chapter 2

Sophia

"Soph?"

I roll my lips between my teeth to keep a grin from taking over my face.

When I first saw this man months ago at the clubhouse, I knew I wanted to see him again. As a soon-to-be-graduating criminal justice major, I had the perfect in.

Detective Colton Matthews stares at me, confused.

I'm not surprised.

I could tell he thought I was someone else mere seconds after I darkened his office door.

He didn't look at me like a charity case, like I was a favor he was doing for my dad.

And I reveled in it.

Then his eyes swept down my body as he took stock of each and every one of my features. That has never happened in this town. Of course I get checked out, I'm young and decent looking. I work out often, so my body type appeals to some people, but the fact that he didn't care who I was when he noticed me standing there meant he in fact didn't know who I was.

The flirting got out of hand. The suggestions got cruder, and if we weren't interrupted by Haden, I imagine we'd be sliding into his car and heading for a nice quiet hotel room.

But, just my luck, I've been figured out.

"Soph?" he repeats after another long pause.

I know his brain must be working ninety to nothing, trying to figure out who exactly I am and going back over our entire conversation word for word as he prepares for the defense against the inappropriate topic we discussed.

"Sophia Anderson," I say as I hold my hand out for him to shake.

"Anderson?"

"Yes." I drop my hand when he makes it clear he isn't going to offer his.

"Dominic Anderson's daughter?"

"Correct." I straighten my suit jacket, growing mildly uncomfortable now that the ruse is over. "I'm here for my internship."

"You were supposed to be here at the beginning of the semester. I expected you in January, not mid-March."

"I had another class I had to finish before I could leave campus." I settle back into the chair across from his desk. "I emailed to let you know I'd be here today."

"Emailed?" His head tilts as his throat works on a swallow. He drops back into his seat, hands shaking the computer mouse to bring his system to life. He focuses on the screen for a long moment before looking back in my direction. "You emailed yesterday."

"Correct." Heat pinks my cheeks, and I hate that he's making me feel like a damn child so soon after our sexual banter mere moments ago.

"That's not very responsible."

"I apologize." The back of my throat burns, but I straighten my back, keeping my eyes locked on the side of his face.

He can't even look at me right now, and I'm certain I've ruined everything. I don't have another internship lined up, and I'm lucky my professor is even allowing this to count as the full credit I need when she didn't have to be so gracious. If I get tossed out of here, I won't graduate on time.

"And you're late because you had to make up another class? Was that also because you flaked on those responsibilities?"

My lips quiver, and I know if I open my mouth to talk about the situation I was in before the holidays last year, I'll cry. There's nothing more cliché than a college girl shedding tears when put on the spot, so I refuse.

I blink at him, mouth clamped closed. Something over my shoulder catches his eye.

He clears his throat and stands from his chair. I mimic his actions. Giving myself permission to break eye contact, I reach down for my computer bag before facing him again.

"I have to meet this professor." He waves his hand, cupping his fingers to someone across the room.

"Do I need to leave?"

His eyes find mine once again, and even though there's still a desk and several feet separating us, I feel small in his presence. Even with respectable three-inch heels on, I feel like he could overpower me if he wanted to, and it's not just his size that intimidates—it's the entire package, the look in his eyes, the way his jaw clenches as he assesses me.

"No, but you will need to change."

"I didn't bring—" My mouth snaps closed when he shifts his weight. "I'll figure it out."

I follow him out of his office, skirting around a middle-aged woman with graying hair.

"Professor Wesley, good morning. Please, have a seat."

The woman greets him cordially. I turn back around to offer a whispered apology, but he closes the door in my face before I can open my mouth.

Deciding to stick around even though I want to run and beg my dad to fix my mistake, I walk out of the police station and head to my car. Dropping my computer bag in the trunk, I mentally go over my options. I can drive back to my parents' house, or I can wear the gym clothes I brought this morning for my evening workout. It'll take well over an hour to go home, get changed, and make it back here. I opt to wear the workout clothes. Besides, I already messed up royally today, so it's not like my apparel could make things worse.

"Things seemed tense in there."

I grimace as I pull the gym bag from the backseat. When I straighten to find Haden standing a few feet away, I want to run through every excuse in the book, but lying to a cop hasn't worked out so far for me today. Yet, the truth isn't an option either. I decide on half and half.

"He wasn't happy with my attire." I shrug. "So, it looks like I'm going to be spending the day in workout gear."

"Can't really chase a perp in heels, Soph."

My eyes widen with the prospect of getting to do some real police work on my first day at interning.

"Really? Think I'll get to tackle a criminal?"

"No." He shakes his head, a genuine smile playing at his lips. "You don't get to rough up perps. Do you honestly think your dad would let you be here if he thought you were in any danger?"

"True." I shrug because arguing with my dad's friend about being a grown woman and able to make my own life choices will only fall on deaf ears.

"Is there a bathroom inside?"

"Let me show you to the women's locker room."

I follow Haden as he opens a side door with an ID card, and less than a minute later, he's standing outside of a heavy door.

"I'll wait here while you change and show you how to get back to Matthews' office."

I make quick work of changing, stashing my gym bag, now filled with the skirt from my business suit I ridiculously thought would make me look more professional. Although I'm sure I look ridiculous, I knew I couldn't spend the day in leggings and a sports bra, so I've kept on the blouse and jacket of my suit, and only replaced my skirt and heels with black leggings and sneakers. I blame police procedural dramas on television for making me think I could do police work in a damn suit and heels.

Haden is on his phone when I exit the locker room, but I follow him when he starts walking. Once we're back in the main office area, he points his finger across the room to a row of four chairs. He gives me a quick wave before disappearing.

My fingers drum on the top of my thighs as I wait for Detective Matthews to exit his office. He can stay in there all day as far as I'm concerned. I figure the longer he's talking to that woman, the better the chance of him not sending me away the second he's done.

"Have you been helped?" I look up to find a handsome man in uniform grinning down at me.

"Hi," I squeak.

"Did you need some help?"

My mouth opens to ask him if he could help with the Detective Matthews situation, but I close it with the ridiculous thought.

"I'm Officer Dillon Ramshaw."

I take his warm hand when he offers it. "Sophia Anderson."

"If you haven't checked in at the front desk, no one will know that you're here." His smile is sweet, his eyes a little more roving than they'd need to be if he only approached me with the purpose of helping.

"I'm waiting for Detective Matthews."

His face falls immediately. "I'm sorry."

I give him a grin of my own at the sincerity in his voice. "Is he a jerk or something?"

His head tilts slightly to the left, confusion apparent on his handsome face. "Are you here about a death?"

"Internship," I answer, barely restraining a mumble about it being over before it even began.

"Ah." His smile returns. "Glad it's not because you've lost someone. He's not a jerk. He's actually a great guy. A little too serious most days, but he works his ass off."

"That's good to know."

"Fuck off, Ramshaw."

Dillon doesn't cringe at Detective Matthews command, and I guess that speaks to the truth he claimed a minute ago about him being a great guy.

"It was nice to meet you, Sophia Anderson."

"You, too, Dillon."

Officer Ramshaw nods at Matthews before strutting away, his hands resting on his utility belt like I've seen many police officers do in the movies.

"Need a napkin for the drool on your chin?"

I narrow my eyes as I stand, trying to get on even ground with Matthews, but I'm now in sneakers, making me even shorter than I was when we first met.

"Jealous?" My throat works on a rough swallow as regret swarms like angry bees in my gut. My mouth—Dad has warned me for years–will be the thing that gets me into trouble every time.

"No reason to be jealous over a boy wanting to—"

"Do the same things to me you wanted to do earlier?" I interrupt, my inability to keep my damn mouth shut continuing.

He crowds my space but somehow still manages not to touch me. I have to crane my head up to keep my eyes locked on his.

"We'll both forget that conversation took place."

Yeah, is that even possible?

"That is if you want to still do this internship."

"It is," I confirm, because the next couple of months are all that stands between me and the rest of my adult life.

"Good. Now let's go. We were expected at a scene ten minutes ago."

Chapter 3

Colton

I'm contemplating my life choices as we leave the police station.

But deep down, I know why I didn't send her away once I realized who she was. Flirting with her, although wildly inappropriate now that it's clear she isn't a college professor, was fun.

Denying that she's sexy as hell, despite knowing she can't be a day over twenty-two, would be useless. Every man in the vicinity is trying to catch her eye, including Ramshaw. He's a decent guy, but sniffing around Dominic Anderson's daughter isn't a very smart thing to do.

Everyone in town knows any female connected to the Cerberus MC is off-limits. We don't even have to be warned. We just all somehow know.

I've always had my concerns about the motorcycle club on the outskirts of town. They're mostly private, only offering bits and pieces of information. Of course, they're extremely active in the community. They help with fundraisers, and I know Monahan could call them for help and they'd show up at any time of day or night, but El Chapo had the respect of the citizens in his community, and we all know that drug dealer wasn't a good guy.

Women in Farmington find their mysterious demeanors attractive, like they're the holy grail of what men should be like. To me, their high level of privacy is suspicious.

"It's locked," Sophia says on the other side of the glass, and I look through the passenger door, wondering when I climbed inside the car and sat down.

I hit the unlock button and wait for her to climb inside.

The fabric of her athletic leggings draw tighter on her thighs, and I try to refocus my attention on something that doesn't have the potential to end with me buried in a shallow desert grave, because honestly, is there a legitimate biker club in existence that is a hundred percent on the right side of the law?

"Detective Matthews?"

I loosen the death grip I have on the steering wheel before looking over at her. She's kept the top part of her outfit on, the thin white fabric hinting at the delicate outline of her bra, and I snap my eyes straight forward again.

"Call me Colton."

"Colton," she repeats, letting the sound play on her tongue.

Big damn mistake.

I clear my throat.

"We're heading across town. A neighbor reported a foul smell, and patrol discovered a deceased person when they went for a wellness check."

"Okay." In my periphery, I see her snapping her seatbelt in place, and it reminds me I need to have mine on as well.

I'm going to have to call Dominic and tell him this just isn't going to work. I can't even climb in the car and head out on a call without getting distracted. My damn job is dangerous, and I don't want to get hurt. I sure as hell don't want to be responsible for this girl—*woman*, my mind reminds me—and her safety.

Maybe I can find someone else in the office that would be willing to take her off my hands. As I put the car in gear and roll out of the parking lot, my mind thinks of Gaffey, but then I remember how I felt when he put his hands on her, and I know that shit won't fly. Granted, he's old enough to be her dad and has worked long enough in the community to know to keep away from her, but Sophia is beyond gorgeous and a temptation to any man that gets hard for the opposite sex.

"Was it back there?" I look at Sophia to see her hitching her thumb over her shoulder.

A quick look in the rearview mirror proves that I can't handle much more of this. The flashing lights of two police cruisers are behind us because I just fucking drove right past the scene we're responding to.

"I want to park on the opposite side of the street," I lie as I pull into an empty driveway and turn around.

A tiny grin plays on her lips as I pull up across the street from the house in question and put the car in park.

"Do you want to stay in the car or come inside?"

I don't know why I'm giving her an option. I know exactly what we're going to be facing in there, and I'd bet there's no quicker way to get her out of my hair than insisting on her tagging along, but for some reason I want to protect her.

"I want to go inside."

"You're sure?" She nods, her eyes looking past my shoulder to take in the activity going on behind me. "There's a dead person in there."

"Correct."

"Have you seen a dead person before?"

"My aunt died when I was twelve."

"Murdered?" I feel a rush of sadness wash over me at the thought of this woman suffering with such a loss.

"Heart failure. She died in her sleep."

This is getting eerily familiar.

"The person in that house probably died in their sleep," I warn, not wanting to trigger her.

"Okay."

"Days ago," I amend.

Her eyes finally meet mine.

"It's cold at night, so the heat in the house has been on. The neighbors called because of the smell."

"Okay."

"You can stay in the car," I offer again.

"Is that where you want me?" There's no sexual inflection to her question, but that doesn't mean that my body knows the difference.

My body wants you under me, a million miles away from the stench of death.

"You're welcome to come inside. I just wanted to warn you, give you a heads-up about what you're going to be walking in on."

"I appreciate that."

She opens her car door when I open mine, and heaven help me, I wait at the front of the car for her to catch up to me. I should regret letting her walk a foot or so ahead of me because my eyes seem to have a mind of their own.

Why in the hell did I have her change her clothes? No skin on her legs is exposed like it was in the skirt, but the leggings peeking out from under the suit jacket are so tight I can't be sure she's wearing underwear.

Jesus, fuck, I'm so screwed.

"Matthews."

I try my best not to frown when I lift my eyes to see Gaffey standing on the front stoop.

"Hey, kiddo."

Sophia gives him a little wave, her jaw clenching with the nickname. It's clear she doesn't like to be seen as a child, and even though I feel the need to correct him because my own thoughts would be illegal if she were an actual kid, I keep my own mouth closed. Demanding he see her as a woman would be showing my hand, and that's the last thing I need.

"It's pretty gruesome in there. Sure you don't want to stay outside?"

"I can handle it." I wish the bravado in her voice would hold up when she's inside, but I know it won't.

"Same as always?" Gaffey asks me. "Ten?"

"Make it twenty," I counter with false faith before turning my attention back to Sophia. "Put gloves on and cover your shoes with those."

I point at the crime scene tech who's holding the supplies, taking my own after she grabs hers. I watch her nose scrunch when a uniformed officer opens the front door. He looks green in the gills, but thankfully he has the wherewithal to get to the other side of his cruiser before losing his breakfast on the asphalt.

"Ready?" I ask Sophia once we're in the proper gear, giving her one more out before we go inside.

"Ready."

Gaffey opens the front door with a flourish, stepping inside quickly as we follow him.

Sophia clears her throat the second we're fully inside, and both Gaffey and I watch her face for signs of getting sick. The smell is god-awful, and I don't know that there's a worse smell in the world than decaying flesh, but she has wide eyes as she looks around the room.

"The deceased is in the master bedroom. Right this way," Gaffey says as he starts to walk down the hallway, sadness hunching his shoulders a little.

Sophia is sandwiched between us as we walk down the narrow hallway, but I don't hear gagging noises come from her as we draw closer to the scene.

"Details?" I ask a uniformed officer as we enter the room.

"Margaret Hanson, seventy-eight. Lives alone. No sign of forced entry. Officers first on the scene had to access the home through a window. Medication in the bathroom indicates she had both heart and kidney problems."

I look over to find Sophia writing all the details in a small notebook. Sweat is beading at her temples, but she doesn't look like she's going to be sick.

"What do you see?" I ask her.

She looks around the room, taking in not only the bed where the deceased is but also looking at the floor, the position of the covers, and the items on the bedside table.

"It all looks… normal."

"She was also on hospice," the original reporting officer adds.

"Natural causes?" Sophia asks, her eyes finding mine.

Before I can answer, the officer who got sick a few minutes ago reappears in the doorway to the room, looking just as ill as he did on his way out earlier.

"Her son is here," he says, his hand covering his mouth.

"I'll be with him in a minute. Why don't you go back outside and wait with him?"

The officer nods, grateful for the reprieve before spinning around and hauling ass out of the house.

"That saliva that's pooling on your tongue is the first sign you're going to puke," Gaffey whispers, and I have to shake my head when I look over to see him leaning in close to whisper in Sophia's ear. The fucker is trying to psych her out. "Can't spit at a scene and swallowing it makes you want to gag."

"Natural causes?" Sophia asks again, ignoring Gaffey.

"Probably," I tell her. "The medical examiner will take all the information we provide and decide if an autopsy is required."

"And the smell of rotting flesh…" Gaffey makes a gagging sound, but Sophia just slowly blinks in his direction. "Do you want some Vicks for your nose?"

"Good cops don't use stuff in their noses. Sometimes the smells coming from the scene can provide hints to the situation the eyes can't see," she says.

My lip twitches, but I manage not to smile.

"Damnit," he mutters as he reaches into his pocket.

"Let's go talk to the family," I say, holding my hand out so Sophia can leave the room first.

"She didn't even flinch," Gaffey complains as he slaps a twenty-dollar bill into my palm.

"She's a badass," I tease, but as I head outside to deliver the bad news, I realize the absolute truth in my words.

Chapter 4

Sophia

"Don't make those gagging noises," I whisper, my throat threatening to close up.

"Really? You're the one going on and on about the smoking hot cop that's old enough to be your dad."

"He's in his mid-thirties. That's not old enough to be my dad."

"Well, he's old enough to be *my* dad."

"Not quite," I argue. "Plus, stop thinking about his age. He's sexy as hell."

Izzy makes another gagging noise, and I nearly lose my dinner.

Keeping it together at that scene earlier was quite possibly the hardest thing I've ever done. When Gaffey started taunting me like he wanted me to get sick, I knew I couldn't cave. I couldn't be a joke or the laughingstock, even though they didn't make fun of the other officer who couldn't handle it.

I wanted to prove something to them, and I think I did. Detective Matthews—Colton as he prefers—was different when we left. His attitude, although not completely gone, was a little more muted than it was before we arrived.

"So, your first dead body, huh?"

It doesn't surprise me that my friend would rather talk about a crime scene than anything resembling romance or sex.

"Really, Izzy?" I shake my head, grinning down at her smiling face on the Facetime video. "I can't talk about it just yet."

Izzy is Hound's daughter, and although I grew up with Gigi, Hound's woman, I'm closer to the former. She's finishing her college semester in Albuquerque, and I already miss her even though we saw each other over spring break last week.

"Let's talk about Colton." I give her a wide smile, batting my eyelashes cartoonishly as I lean back against my headboard.

"Colton? First name basis, must be serious," she deadpans.

I huff a laugh at her lack of enthusiasm. "Iz! He's got muscles for days. His five o'clock shadow would make angels weep."

"He sounds old."

"He's majestic and so tall."

"You're short," she reminds me. "Everyone is tall to you."

"Can you just hop on the Colton-Matthews-is-the-sexiest-man-alive train with me for ten minutes?"

If she doesn't approve of my crush, then there's no sense in even mentioning what happened during the case of mistaken identity first thing this morning.

"Choo-choo." She smiles as she pumps her arm up and down like a train conductor.

"Better." I grin into the camera.

"Are you going to keep flirting with him? Because that may make things weird while you're working together."

"I—" I snap my jaw closed because we've promised each other we'd always be honest. We get too many half-truths from the people in our lives under the auspices of protecting us. "I probably shouldn't. I have to graduate on time."

"True. Plus, you're used to being around hot guys. He's no different."

I couldn't even explain my attraction to Colton out loud without sounding like a fawning teen. Yeah, the man is possibly the hottest creature I've ever seen, but there's just something else about him that makes me want to inch in closer to him, to crawl inside his head and figure out what he's thinking.

"Professional," I muse.

"I think that's best. I know there are a couple guys on campus who are going to miss you."

"That part of my life is over," I explain.

"Over? Like dating?"

"Dating college guys," I clarify.

"Who else will you date? And don't tell me Detective Colton Matthews because he's not an option."

"I'll have to date, eventually."

"Not in Farmington you won't."

"He's going to have to let me date eventually," I argue.

"When you're thirty, like Jasmine."

God, she's right. My older sister didn't introduce a man to my dad until she was out of her twenties. She led a wild life, going to sex clubs and having a good time, much like I've done for the last four years at college, but I don't want to have to move away to find a life. My family is here in Farmington. It's where I want to work, and where I want to eventually raise a family.

"I'm not going back to college boys."

"You mean boys your age?"

We both laugh because it's true. I'm not quite twenty-two, but boys my age no longer appeal to me, and this isn't new information since meeting Colton. I haven't really wanted drunken parties and fumbling boys for a while now.

"College boys are terrible at sex."

Izzy clears her throat.

"Like they seriously can't even find the clit."

She chokes on nothing, and I grin watching her cheeks pink up in embarrassment.

I don't have a lot of experience, but she has even less. I'm not sure she's even lost her virginity yet.

I'd ask, but she'd give me the runaround. I don't know how she was born to very young parents and still has all of these hang-ups about sex.

Me, on the other hand, I'm what she likes to call devilish, but really it's mostly all talk. I'm not a virgin, having given that prize drunkenly away at a frat party to a douche named Chad. He didn't stick around, but that's on me because *Chad*, really? Enough said. My dalliances since haven't been anything to write home about. Nonetheless, I'm mostly all talk. The bravado I managed to hold onto in Colton's office was all talk, much like my complaints on college boys being bad at sex. I don't really know how to please a man either, but at least I'm willing to try.

Footfalls in the hall draw my attention.

"And the blush was on sale too. You should check them out online," I'm saying when my bedroom door swings open.

I look over to see my dad as Izzy speaks without missing a beat. "But what about the foundation because mine is almost out. Figure I should grab both while I'm there. Do you have any coupons?"

Code for *how long is this going to take*.

"I have one in my email I'm not going to use. I'll send it over to you. Tell Dad, hi." I turn my phone around so Izzy can wave at my father who even nearly twenty-two years later still doesn't knock on my bedroom door.

"Hi, Mr. Anderson."

"Call me, Dom, Izzy. How many times do I have to tell you?"

Izzy laughs, but doesn't speak to him again. "I have to study for that political science test. I'll be waiting on the coupon."

Code for *call me when he leaves, we aren't done discussing this.*
"Bye. I'll send it over shortly."
Code for *as soon as I can get rid of him, I'll call you back.*
We end the call, and I give my dad all of my attention.

I love this man. Honestly, he's my hero. He kissed every scratch, held me when my sister, Jasmine's, dog died, but he hasn't let me experience much life outside of the clubhouse and school. I blame his twenty years in the Marine Corps, along with his work with Cerberus for being overprotective. He does it out of love, but it's smothering.

That's why I need the internship with Colton to work out because once I graduate, I'll be able to get a real job and have the ability to move out. Besides, he needs to put more focus on my sister and what she's doing rather than sticking his nose in my business. So I have a crush on an older guy. Jasmine is living with two men, as in they're all three in a relationship.

My dad didn't want me driving to work alone this morning, but he hardly blinked an eye at her news. Granted, she's over thirty, but get your priorities straight, man. This is Farmington, and nothing seriously bad ever happens here.

"Mom mentioned you needed different clothes for work." Dad holds up a bag I'm only now noticing. "I talked with Monahan and he's going to have some shirts for you tomorrow."

"Thanks, Dad." I take the bag and pull out several pairs of khaki-colored utility pants, running my fingers over the waffle-like texture of the fabric.

"I honestly don't see the need for those type of pants. It's not like office work on fraud cases really require it."

"Fraud cases? Dad, really? I saw my first dead body today. It was absolutely disgusting, and the smell nearly made me puke, but I didn't."

"Dead body?" He inches closer as if he has the ability to protect me now, after the fact. His fingers shove into his pocket. "Matthews works fraud."

"He's a homicide detective," I correct.

"Is that so?" His voice has an edge to it I haven't heard since he caught me sneaking back into the house late one night and tried to convince him I was at a study group.

"Yes." I straighten my spine, worried that he's going to do something to compromise my internship. "And I want to keep working there. I only have two months left of school. If you do something to make me lose my internship, I'll never forgive you."

He frowns. "That's a little dramatic don't you think? I'm just going to see if I can get you moved to a department that isn't going to give you nightmares."

"Dad!" I hiss, but he spins around and leaves the room.

I follow him, unwilling to just let him plow through another situation in my life.

"Do not call the police station."

"Police station?" Mom asks when we make it into the kitchen. "Do we need to go to the panic room?"

I know there's a safe room in their closet, but we've never had to use it once since I've been born.

Mom smiles at me, and I have to roll my eyes. She tries to be on my side, knowing that keeping us locked down will only cause problems later in life. *They have to experience things*, she argued once, but her defense fell on deaf ears.

"He's trying to ruin my life," I whine.

She turns back around, continuing to wash vegetables in the sink. "Is that so, or are you being dramatic?"

Okay, so neither my dad nor I are perfect.

"He's upset that I'm interning with the homicide detective."

That news is enough to make her turn off the water and dry her hands.

"He's going to force me to work with the fraud guy."

"Matthews is supposed to be the fraud guy," Dad argues, but at least his phone is back in his damn pocket.

"Matthews? Isn't he that cute detective working with Jinx and Rocker?"

"He's working with Simone Murphy," I correct, knowing that much from the gossip around the clubhouse.

The situation is more complicated, but the gist is that Simone killed her abusive ex and is now pregnant with either Jinx or Rocker's baby. I don't know if paternity has been determined yet.

"Cute?" Dad asks, focusing on his wife.

The rumble of his voice is a challenging hint at foreplay, and as much as I want to cringe and crawl away, I have to stand my ground on this one. Growing up with parents with mass amounts of sexually charged energy has been both a blessing and a curse. A blessing because it showed Jasmine and I exactly what we should aim for—a man that only has sights for one woman and doesn't have a problem showing her how he feels. The curse because they're my parents. So seriously... gross.

"Mom!" I groan when she starts to bite her lip with her eyes on my dad. "Can you get it under control for a few minutes? Tell him not to call the station to rearrange my internship."

"Don't rearrange her internship," my mother says.

"She saw a damn dead body today," Dad argues, and this is one of the few times I want him more concerned about the chance of getting my mom naked than focused on me.

I shudder and refocus on my dad.

"Really?" Mom's voice grows softer, and I can tell she's looking at me, but I can't face her right now.

The man outside of that house this morning was devastated, and it didn't matter that he was grown and had adult children of his own. Losing a parent can't be easy at any age.

Emotion clogs my throat with the memory because there's just something heartbreaking about seeing a man cry.

"Are you okay?"

She inches closer to me, arms out as if she wants to wrap me in a hug.

"I'm fine." I step away, putting the kitchen island between us.

I'll break down if she touches me, and I have to be stronger than that if I want Dad to take me seriously.

"I know you want to protect her from everything in the world, but you also raised her to think independently and not to rely on anyone." Mom is speaking to Dad now so I let some of the tension in my shoulders fall. "You can't change that opinion now that she's finally doing it."

I'm both happy and sad with her words because I know it's part truth, part jab. I'm standing here arguing about my freedom of choice, but I also needed new clothes to wear to work. Instead of going to the store and getting them myself, I called my mom to fix the dilemma. Apparently, I have one foot in and one foot out, and gaining my own autonomy isn't possible this way.

Chapter 5

Colton

I was awake before the alarm clock went off this morning, drinking coffee in the kitchen before the sun even thought about starting the day. It has nothing to do with being eager to go to work, and nothing to do with getting to spend another day with Sophia Anderson.

I can't have those thoughts.

They're not allowed.

I can't think about the way her flowery scent filled the car yesterday or predicting what she's going to wear to work today.

Nope.

None of that is allowed.

Shouldn't even be in my head.

So that definitely means I should stop thinking about her mouth.

I shouldn't have spent my morning shower concocting ways to get in her space today.

I should probably erase all curiosities about what her hair would feel like sifting through my fingertips.

And I sure as shit shouldn't speculate the types of sounds she'd make when I—

My ringing phone startles me, making me wonder how I got halfway to work without a single memory of even pulling out of my driveway.

"Matthews," I snap after answering the call through my truck's Bluetooth.

"Sophia was ecstatic about her first day working with you."

I nearly rear end the car in front of me as it slows for a red light.

"That so?"

Great, man. Way to sound casual. I swallow wondering if he heard the crack in my voice.

Silence fills the cab of the truck, but I wait him out.

"Something you need to tell me?"

Aw fuck. Surely, she didn't go home and tell him every damn thing.

"Sophia handled herself very well yesterday. I won a twenty-dollar bet."

More silence.

"You should be proud of her."

Silence.

I clamp my jaw closed, pressing on the gas a little too hard when the light turns green and the car behind me honks.

I'm not going to say another damn word. I'm a cop for fuck's sake. I know exactly what he's doing. This shit isn't going to work on me.

"That's not what I'm talking about."

I return the silence when he doesn't elaborate.

Why does it feel like an admission of guilt? Would this man understand if he knew I thought she was someone else?

And the thoughts you had about her after her identity was revealed?

The tires on my truck screech when I pull up to the police station, the pressure from my brakes too much for the situation. One of the patrol officers looks my way, but I wave off his concern.

"You're no longer working fraud."

"I've been on homicide for the last year."

"You didn't tell me that when we talked in November."

"You didn't ask."

A rush of air comes through the line, and I can't determine if it's a growl of anger or a chuckle. I don't know enough about the man to make an educated guess either.

"I've worked the Simone Murphy case. I thought you knew that."

"I thought you were just helping out with that."

"Nope. All deaths land on my desk."

He grows silent once again, and as much as I want to wait him out again, I just can't seem to manage it.

"The case yesterday was an elderly woman who died in her sleep. The horrific part was she was there for a couple of days. Sophia didn't even blink."

It makes me wonder what her childhood was like that a decaying body didn't cause more of a reaction.

"She's strong, even one of the beat cops got sick... twice."

"She's a great kid."

I do my best to ignore the skeevy feeling his declaration causes, but I don't really see her as a kid. I mean, how could I? Other than her father and other family members, I don't think there's a man alive that wouldn't give her a second glance, and that makes my jaw ache with tension at the thought of her at the MC clubhouse.

"Let me know if she starts to cause problems."

I'm certain this man isn't interested in hearing about the perpetual hard-on she's going to cause for the next couple of months.

"Will do," I assure him before hanging up.

I sit in the truck a little longer, questioning my sanity because although I wanted to move her to a different division yesterday, I can't imagine doing that now.

Telling by the questions she asked about the case yesterday, she's intelligent. She caught on amazingly fast with the system we used after offering to help type up my handwritten notes. She didn't flirt or mention our introductions.

I mean, it didn't stop my eyes from taking her in or my thoughts from speeding out the front door of the police station and landing in a dark room at the Hampton Inn, but at least I can keep my distance if she doesn't hint at wanting to hook up.

I walk into the building, eyes assessing, seeing who's here, and although I'm nearly an hour early, I find Sophia in my office looking through the paperback version of this year's traffic code.

"Interesting reading?" I ask, slipping around my desk and placing my coffee cup near my computer monitor.

"Not really." She closes the book before looking up at me.

Her hair isn't in a tight knot on the back of her head like it was yesterday. For all the sexy librarian vibes I got yesterday, make that tenfold for the head cheerleader thoughts the ponytail is giving me right now. I dated a head cheerleader once, and she managed to change my entire life trajectory.

Won't be making that mistake again.

Not that Sophia was a cheerleader at any point in her life. Just after the ten-minute call with her dad, I can't picture the man letting her put on a short skirt and bounce around for hundreds of men in the stands, but hell if I can't get lost in the imagery.

"What is it?" Her grin is casual with no hints of the seduction the woman used yesterday morning.

"Were you a cheerleader in high school? College?"

Her head snaps back a little. "What? No."

"Think cheerleading is dumb?" I break eye contact, wiggling my mouse to wake up my computer.

"Too much work. Do you know how much time cheerleaders spend training? Yeah, that's not for me."

I keep my eyes on my screen. I'm not disappointed so much as remembering what she said yesterday about falling behind in her classes. Despite her enthusiasm yesterday, I expect her to lose interest in this internship quickly. Maybe she's good at putting on a front, but if there's one thing I know, it's that people who aren't willing to accept any level of responsibility don't stick around for long.

The grass is always greener after all.

"I'm going to go get a coffee refill." Sophia places the traffic code on the corner of my desk before standing. "Can I get you anything?"

"Nope," I say without looking in her direction.

"Be right back."

But she doesn't come right back. I sit in my office for twenty minutes before going to look for her. I don't know what I was expecting to find, but her in the breakroom surrounded by smiling, horny cops isn't too much of a surprise.

I stand off to the side for a few minutes watching the interactions, and it gives me the opportunity to get a good look at her. She isn't in a sexy, little pencil skirt or athletic leggings. Today, she's got on khaki utility pants, much like the guys in the criminal investigation division wear. Those aren't the issue, nor is it really what's causing all the dogs on the force to come sniffing around. I mean, it may contribute, but I haven't seen her from the back yet.

What's drawing all the attention—or at least mine anyway—is the tight, sweat-wicking fabric of her shirt. It may be department issued, with the Farmington PD logo just above her left breast, but there isn't a soul I've met that could pull it off the way she is right now. Let me just say, if she had lace on her bra, the men standing close to her would be able to count the eyelets in the pattern.

"Yeah, I get off at seven this evening," Dresden says as I walk closer. "But we could definitely see about a ride-along later in the week."

Sophia catches sight of me over the man's shoulder, and instantly I can tell her genuine smile—the one she's giving me—versus the polite one she's been giving Dresden.

"How's Emily and the baby, Pete? Little Ava is what, two weeks old now?"

Dresden spins, giving me a lethal look. "Four weeks, tomorrow."

Without another word, Dresden begins to walk away. Several of the other guys, many loitering but not brave enough to approach her, begin shouting comments about him being a dick and how his wife deserves better.

"Really?" Sophia asks as she begins to follow me back to my office. "He's married with a newborn?"

"Men are dogs," I respond automatically. "You're twenty-two, you should know that by now."

"In three months."

"Hmm?" I plop back down in my office chair, already exhausted when the day is just getting started. Tossing and turning last night isn't doing me any favors today.

"I'll be twenty-two in three months. How many of those guys out there are married?" She takes the seat across from me, but she ignores the traffic code on the corner of my desk.

"Most of them, either that or they're divorced." I study her when she frowns. "Dresden's marriage won't last either but I wouldn't suggest getting in the middle of it right now."

"I wouldn't," she snaps, sounding offended. "So, there's a high divorce rate among police officers?"

I can't stop the snort that leaves my nose. "The first thing the training officer told my class during the academy was to get the first marriage out of the way."

"Really?" Her cute little nose scrunches up as if she's disgusted.

"I take it your parents are still together?"

"Aren't yours?"

"Well, yeah, but my dad isn't a cop."

She nods, conceding the fact, but she still looks curious. "How old are you?"

"Old enough."

"Yet acting twelve with that response." She leans back in her chair, arms crossed over her stomach, and fuck, that damn shirt is going to be the death of me.

"Thirty-five, and before you have the chance to ask, I was divorced before I was old enough to even go into the police academy."

I turn my attention back to the stack of cases on my desk, shuffling through them until I find the one that needs to be worked on today.

"What?"

"We have everything we need to clear this case today, but I'd like you to look through it and see if there's anything that catches your eye." I offer her the folder, effectively shutting down whatever questions she could want to ask next.

I keep my work and personal life separate for a reason, and I don't plan on changing that anytime soon.

"A drunk driving accident?" she asks, but her eyes keep scanning the file. "Isn't this open and shut? The man blew a point two-nine at the scene. By the time he got to the hospital for the blood draw it was even higher. Oh God. The entire family?" Emotion clogs her throat, but for some reason it calms me.

I lost sleep last night questioning her lack of response to the scene with the elderly woman yesterday.

"The mother, father, and their four-year-old son," I confirm. "They were on their way back from a playdate."

"This is awful."

"The worst. Ramshaw was the first on the scene. He's a stronger man than me."

"Was he able to hold it together?"

I shake my head, dropping my eyes to my desk when she looks up at me. Man, people hurting kids. It's just something I have serious trouble dealing with.

"He worked the scene. Gave the breathalyzer. Handcuffed the man. Made sure to transport the drunk driver to the hospital to get everything we would need to make sure he's locked away for a long time."

"Isn't that what he's supposed to do?" I nod. "But not what you would've done?"

I lift my eyes to hers. "I would have unloaded both my magazines into him."

She looks back down to the folder, brushing a tear off her cheek. There was no judgment, no disappointment on her face before she broke eye contact.

"He's twenty," she gasps.

"In his statement, he said he was too scared to call someone for a ride. Since he's underage, he knew his parents would lose their shit about him drinking. He decided to take the chance."

"My dad would be livid if I called home drunk and needed a ride home," she whispers. "But I still wouldn't get behind the wheel of a car. How selfish."

"Who would you call?" I ask.

"Anyone but Dad." She looks up, winking at me, and the sadness filling the office fades away. "Who would you have called?"

"If I were that young and in trouble?" She nods. "My dad. It wouldn't be the first time he had to bail me out of a life changing situation. Do you drink often?"

It's a college student's rite of passage, right? I mean, I wouldn't know because my college courses were taken several years after high school graduation, and responsibilities kept me from living that type of life.

"Not really. I mean, I can have a couple beers at the clubhouse, but there's always a bed to crash in or someone able to take me back home."

A bed to crash in. Why does that sentence bring up a little green monster?

"I can't get drunk."

"Never? Didn't you go away for college?"

"Albuquerque," she confirms. "And what Daddy doesn't know, doesn't hurt him."

Another wink.

Another erection I'm going to have to talk down before I can stand from this desk.

"If you're ever in the situation and need a ride, you can always call me."

"I don't have your number."

I pull a pen from the cup on my desk and scribble out my number before offering her the slip of paper. That was the first step I made on my journey to ruin this girl's life.

Chapter 6

Sophia

"You've been a huge help these last couple of weeks."

I give Colton a weak smile.

"Seriously. My desk is nearly cleaned off, and that's thanks to you."

"Most of those cases just needed to be typed up and submitted to records," I remind him.

"And now you know my greatest weakness."

"Follow through?" I tease, but snap my mouth closed when I realize how provocative it sounded.

He coughs a laugh into his hand. "Yeah."

"What happens next?" I ask, tilting my face toward the window but still unable to take a full breath.

The man smells amazing, always does. I even find myself sniffing my clothes when I get home to see if by chance it's somehow permeated my own clothes. I come up empty-handed every time, but it doesn't stop me from checking.

I've been doing this internship for the last three weeks, and I've managed to stop biting my lip when he walks by. Some days, I can even carry on a conversation without staring at his mouth. Twice this week alone, he was able to get up and leave his office and I didn't follow him with my eyes all the way out the door, but I'm feeling exceptionally weak where he's concerned today. Maybe it was the dream I had last night or the haircut he got after work yesterday, but he's managed to land right back on my radar, and I'm struggling.

Hitting the button for the window, I lean my head a little further away, hoping for a breath of fresh air that isn't tinged with the spicy scent of his cologne.

"Hot?"

Burning up.

"Struggling a little today," I confess, but then think better of telling the full truth. "That last scene was a bit much."

"Worse than the SIDS case we worked on Tuesday?"

"Somehow," I answer, rolling my head on the back of the seat to look at him. "I don't think there was much more the parents could've done for that baby."

I cried so much Tuesday night that layers of makeup couldn't hide my puffy eyes the next day. I clear my throat, knowing the tears will start back up if I let myself focus on that family's loss.

"I understand. Someone could've helped that young woman today. It was clear by the track marks on her arms and the filth she was living in that today wasn't her first time to shoot heroin."

"Exactly," I whisper, emotion clogging my throat. "How many people saw her and didn't help? Had her parents done anything to try to get her clean?"

"Both good questions," he answers. "We're heading to her mother's house now, and I can tell you by the address given that there's a good chance the answer is going to be that she didn't get help because her parents aren't able to help themselves. Many addicts also have family members that are also on drugs. Not all, mind you, but some."

"And this woman we're going to go see?"

"Has had numerous arrests for drug possession. Has been to prison more than once because of them."

"That's sad."

"It's a vicious cycle, and some people are wound so tight up in it that no amount of help will set them free."

"She was only seventeen."

"Heartbreaking," he mutters, and it makes me want to go home and reach out to Landon.

Dustin "Kid" Andrews' son is the youngest one around, not counting Gigi's daughter, and he had to have known this girl. Farmington isn't an overly large community.

"Here?" I ask when Colton pulls into the back part of a parking lot.

I can't handle this right now. Leaving that crack house with the sight of that girl's vomit-covered blue lips is burned into my brain, and I need to keep myself busy to keep from thinking about it.

"I want you to look at this."

I barely register the brush of his hand on my leg when he reaches for the lock on the glovebox, but the sensation skates up my leg anyway. Maybe it's the proximity of him that's frying my brain, or my need to always be tough and strong around him. I don't know what it is, but I'm grateful it's Friday and I have two days Colton-free to get my head back on straight.

He reaches into the glovebox, shuffling the papers around until he pulls his hand free.

"A pamphlet?" I ask when he lays the tri-fold paper in my lap without touching me further. "Notifying next of kin?"

I look at the dull, faded information sheet, briefly going through the bullet points of the best practices when notifying someone that a person they love is deceased.

"Really?" I look up at him to find a faraway look in his eyes. "This is the training a cop gets to help tell a mother that her daughter is never coming home again? That she'll never see her smile or hear her laugh ever again."

"Sophia."

"No," I snap. "This is ridiculous. A child is gone and the department hands this to someone, expecting them to deliver the worst news a person is ever going to hear."

I freeze when he brushes his fingers under my eyes and they come away wet.

"Fuck," I mutter, untucking my shirt and lifting the hem of it to dry my face.

He reaches past me again, grabbing a few fast-food napkins from the glovebox and shoving them my way. "This is better, put your shirt down."

I don't even have the strength right now to feel embarrassed that I may have just flashed this man the bottom curve of my bra-covered breasts. I mean, who even cares at this point.

"That pamphlet is a guideline, a reminder that even when giving bad news, we have to be diligent and observant. Not all notifications are simple and straight forward. Sometimes we're walking into a situation where the person being notified already knows what happened because they were the perp." I stiffen at his words. "Notifications never get easier, and there's nothing on that card that can prepare you for the grief a person feels, but it's helpful to look at so that the officer is cognizant that they have a job to do."

I flip the pamphlet over, feeling a little better for the hotline numbers on the back for police officers to call. First responders see so much brutality and pain. It's no wonder they burnout quickly, commit suicide, and have trust issues. They're dealing with some of the worst situations the world can dream up. Take today for example. Three hours ago, we were in the office going through cases and debating our equality staunch stances on *The Office* versus *New Girl*—I'm team Zoey Deschanel all the way—when we were called out to work the case of a dead seventeen-year-old overdose victim. It's like zero to a hundred in the blink of an eye, and although I've only been helping out for a few weeks, it's already taking its toll on me.

"Soph?"

I pull my eyes from the paper in my hands to look at him.

"If this is too much for you—"

"I'm fine." His jaw clenches.

"You don't have to be strong in front of me."

If only that were true.

"So, we're looking at the situation from the outside, assessing the entire scene as if it were an open investigation?" I ask, changing the subject because I've been vulnerable enough for one day. Hell, to last a lifetime as far as I'm concerned.

"It's good practice. The narcotics team will help with this investigation to see if they can get any leads to dealers, but I don't expect them to get far. The house has been abandoned for years. People have been squatting in there. You saw the condition of the place. I wouldn't doubt that they could pull over a hundred different DNA samples from that carpet."

I cringe at the reminder. That young girl died in solid filth on a threadbare mattress, all alone.

"Are you ready?"

"I'm just observing, right?"

"Of course. I'll do all the talking."

I shove the pamphlet back in the glovebox, wipe my face with the napkins one more time, and focus my attention out through the windshield. When I take a deep breath, I'm once again overwhelmed with the rich scent of him, only this time I breathe in deeply and hold that part of him in my lungs.

Too soon, less than three minutes to be exact, we're pulling up in front of a rundown duplex with boarded-up windows.

"Someone lives here?" I ask, nose to the glass, but still uncertain about getting out of the car.

"Destiny's mother does. Well, it's her last known address." He opens his car door, but my hand hesitates on my door handle. "You can stay in the car if you want."

Instead of taking him up on his offer, I shove open my door. He gives a quick grin, and I can tell he's impressed with my resiliency. What he doesn't know is tonight will be another night I cry myself to sleep, all the while being grateful for the life I've been allowed to live, including my overprotective, overbearing dad who I can see now has only ever wanted what's best for me by keeping me safe and protecting me from the ugliness that seems to be infecting the world.

"Keep your eyes open," he reminds me as we make our way up the cracked concrete walkway.

His hand goes to my back to steady me when I catch the toe of my boot on the uneven terrain.

"Careful."

"Sorry," I mutter.

"You good?"

Before I can answer, the door on the right of the duplex swings open, the screen door hitting the side of the house with a loud crack.

"Matthews," the woman standing in the doorway grunts as we approach.

I don't make a sound when he steps in front of me. Any other day I might get mad, but this is a neighborhood I was never allowed in, and although at the time I thought my parents were being elitist jerks, I can see clearly they had their reasons.

A car alarm goes off down the street, inciting several unruly dogs to begin barking, but the woman in front of us doesn't blink an eye or look in the direction of the noise. No one else opens their doors, no curtains flutter from curiosity within. I don't imagine someone calling for help would draw much attention, and definitely not someone willing to offer a helping hand.

"Doris," Colton says as we draw closer. He stops several feet away, and I use the opportunity to take in all the information that I can.

This woman doesn't seem nervous, but more annoyed that we're interrupting her day. Her fingers flex in and out several times before she lifts a hand to scratch at an already irritated spot on her arm.

"Who's the new trainee? She looks a little young to be a detective."

"I'm here to talk about Destiny, Doris."

"She took off again. I told social services last week I didn't know where that damn girl is. You know they're trying to take me to court because she isn't going to school. I told that lady that she refuses to go, and the last time I tried to make her, she hit me in the face. Did social services tell you that? I'm not going to jail over her again."

"Doris—"

"Ever since she took off with Hershel, she's been a different kid." Her jaw works back and forth between her words, and it doesn't take a rocket scientist to deduce this woman has had her own struggles with drugs. Although not as filthy as we found her deceased daughter, it's clear it's been a couple of days since she's seen the inside of a shower. It makes me wonder if she has running water, another thing I've always taken for granted.

"Doris—"

"I won't. I'm not going to jail!" she screeches, her bony arms crossing over her chest with defiance.

"Police were called out to the abandoned house over on the hill."

Doris swallows, and I can see it in her eyes when she realizes why we're here. We don't even have to say the words, and this woman is already cycling through the stages of grief.

Tears burn the backs of my eyes because despite all that's going on, this woman has lost a child.

"She's dead?" Her chin quivers heavily.

"She is. An overdose is suspected, but it'll take some time before toxicology comes back."

"Was Hershel there?"

"She was alone in the house, Doris. Someone called into the anonymous tip line."

Tears roll down Doris's cheeks, but she doesn't crumple the way I believed she would at the news. Her affect is a little flat, but it's clear she's hurting.

"Gone? She's gone?"

"Yes, ma'am. I'm so sorry for your loss. Detective Winston will probably be by in the next week or so. He's going to have some questions about who she's been hanging out with."

"I'm not telling him shit," she snaps.

Colton nods his head in understanding before reaching into his shirt pocket for a business card. "There's a number for a grief hotline on the back, Doris. Call them if you need someone to talk to."

She snaps the card out of his hand, ignoring it when it flutters to the ground.

"Did she have any money on her?"

My head snaps in her direction, but it's the clench in Colton's strong jaw that garners most of my attention.

"She didn't have any possessions on her, Doris."

"Personal effects can be picked up at the coroner's office, right?"

There's no talking sense into this woman, and it's clear this isn't her first notification.

"Yes, ma'am. Give them a couple days, and you can pick up anything she had."

We turn to leave. Colton crowds me but not a single part of his body brushes mine as we walk back to the car, and it sucks because I feel like I need some form of comfort after today. I don't know that I have the strength to do this all over again on Monday.

Chapter 7

Colton

"Sometimes those are harder to deal with than brutal murders," I say after sitting in the car for ten minutes outside of the station.

Sophia is still looking out the side window, making no move to get out of the car.

"She didn't care."

"She cared," I counter. "She's just too far gone to feel the real pain of her loss. She may spend the next two years with a needle in her arm to keep from feeling that pain."

"Denial," she whispers.

"Addict," I argue. "It's much worse."

"That girl deserved much better."

"Doris deserves better, too."

"I don't see it."

She hasn't looked at me once since we walked back to our car, leaving Doris to deal with her grief the only way she knew how.

"Destiny was a toddler the first time I dealt with her mother. Doris was drunk one night at a bar in town and left her kid in the car. Destiny was never one to stay still, and someone called it in that they found a kid walking down the road in the middle of the night. My partner at the time wasn't surprised. He knew exactly who the kid was and who she belonged to. We drove straight to the bar after making sure the kid was safe with social services."

I have to look out my window to get a better handle on my own anger. There are so many situations I wish were different in my career as a police officer.

"They gave her back to her mother?"

"There are circumstances. Years ago, Doris worked very hard to comply with the courts."

"Circumstances?" She finally jerks her head in my direction, and the hatred for what she saw today is so much better than the tears she cried in the parking lot earlier.

"Not everyone gets to grow up in a two-parent household with love."

She blinks at me. "I won't be shamed for having a healthy childhood."

I want to ask her if she really did, but I can tell by the look in her eyes that the man that raised her kept her safe. The experiences we've faced in this job together has opened her eyes to the terrible things that are possible so close to home.

Over the last couple of weeks, the wondering I had going on about what really happens at the Cerberus MC clubhouse has been laid to rest. Her reaction at the very first crime scene was a hundred percent bravado, and it wouldn't surprise me if I found out later that she went home and got sick more than once.

"I'm glad you had a healthy childhood." I grip the steering wheel because that pressure under my palms is the only thing keeping me from reaching for her and brushing my fingertips down the side of her face. "Doris didn't have a good childhood."

"Neither did Destiny," she counters. "Hell, that girl probably didn't have a childhood at all."

"Doris was raped by her father from the time she was seven years old until she ran away at fifteen. She was pregnant with Destiny when she left."

"What?" A trembling hand lifts to cover her mouth, but it doesn't stop the anguished sob from escaping.

"There are circumstances all over this community. Nothing is cut and dry. Everyone has a story, some worse than others. You'll learn if you work in the criminal justice field long enough that every situation is different. Some people make it out of shitty situations, and some people are born with no chance at all. Sometimes horrible things happen to good people. But most importantly, you'll come to understand that most often, there's no rhyme or reason. You saw two families change this week with the loss of a child. Two families that will never be the same, and no matter the individual situation, two mothers will close their eyes tonight with another piece of their soul missing."

"But some people make it out," she whispers, holding on to the good, and that's one of the things I admire most about this woman.

"Yes." I open my mouth to share a little more truth, but she doesn't need to know that the ones like us that grow up in homes where we were loved tend to have the most compassion for those who didn't. It's the ones who pulled themselves out of shitty situations, most often, that have less than stellar attitudes about those still stuck by their circumstances. Maybe it's because they made it out, they stop seeing excuses the same way. I don't know what it is, but everyone deals with police work differently.

"I'm just glad it's the weeks' end."

Glassy eyes blink up at me, and my mouth opens before I think. I don't want her going home for two days with all of this heaviness weighing on her. She'll soon find out that each day in this job, a little piece of you is plucked away and never returned. She's too young to be jaded by the evils in the world.

"What are you doing this evening?"

"Besides going home and hugging my mom and dad?" She chuckles, the sound sullen and humorless.

"What about dinner?"

"Mom usually leaves me a plate in the oven."

I smile at her confession even though her cheeks pink.

"I know how to cook, and I was on my own for almost four years at college. I mean, I was in a dorm, but I'm not a spoiled brat who can't take care of myself."

I press a hand to her arm to get her attention and stop her rambling, but pull it away before she can read it as anything else. God, I want my hands all over her. I clear my throat.

"My mom still brings over meals, and I'm thirty-five. I'm pretty sure I have enough casseroles in my freezer to survive a zombie apocalypse."

She grins at me, but the smile I saw earlier today in my office is still absent.

"Will you join me?"

"For what?"

I chuckle, shaking my head and looking out my window after realizing the way I asked about dinner wasn't taken as the invitation it was meant to be.

"Will you have dinner with me?"

Her eyes widen, and more of her beautiful smile takes over her face.

"I mean as a reward for going back into the office and helping me wrap a few things up?"

"Of course there's a catch."

"I'm not on call this weekend, but I'll end up at my desk tomorrow morning if I leave stuff undone."

"Really?" She licks her lips, and I'm snared by the action. "Last week I helped close out a case that was lost under a pile for the last four months."

"See." I hold my hands up in offering. "I need your help."

"I'll warn you, I eat a lot."

I laugh again. "I know. I've seen your lunch orders. Come on."

I slide out of the car, making sure to grab my gear since I'll leave the vehicle here for the weekend, and head inside before she has the chance to change her mind.

***

"Please don't tell me you're counting calories."

I glare at Sophia as she looks down at her plate of pasta, her mouth working back and forth.

"What? No." She leans across the table, lowering her head as if she's going to tell me a secret. "But would it be rude to ask for more cheese?"

I laugh, but then she winks at me and the sound dies on my lips.

I know she isn't flirting. She's been nothing but professional. The last couple of weeks have been easygoing when I would've put money on the chance of it being difficult to be around her.

I mean, some days it isn't easy, and those are the days she wears her hair down around her shoulders, and I spend the entire shift trying to keep from reaching out to touch her brown locks.

Today is one of those days. Her grin is enticing, but add in the soft waves flowing around her face and shoulders, and I can now see that inviting her out while not working in an official capacity may have been a mistake.

"Do you really want more cheese?" I ask when my brain decides to finally come back online.

"Of course not." Those are her words, but her eyes dart around the restaurant.

We eat in silence for the next couple of minutes, and her cheeks flame red when the waiter stops by to check on us and I ask for more cheese. She must not be too upset because her eyes go wide and it takes forever to tell him that's enough when the grater starts working.

"This is so good," she mumbles, her mouth half full as she shovels more linguini into her pretty mouth.

"The best," I say, but I'm only partially talking about the meal. "Tell me about growing up at the clubhouse."

"I didn't," she says, covering her mouth with her cloth napkin as she finishes chewing. "My mom and dad never lived on the property. They have a house out on the lake."

"But you spent a lot of time there?"

"We were there all the time. We still spend a lot of time there."

"And there are a lot of men around?" Jesus, why did I ask that fucking question? "I mean the guys that work for Kincaid."

"Diego is my uncle." She narrows her eyes, ready to defend him the second my mouth opens to offer something inflammatory.

"Everyone at the station loves him. He helps the community a ton."

"I had thousands of community service hours by the time I graduated."

If that's the case, I'm surprised I never saw her until she walked into my office, but my homelife the last decade and a half hasn't really left much time for extracurriculars.

"And you hated it?"

"Not even close. I spent a lot of time at the animal shelter. Sunday afternoons we spent many hours at the assisted-living home. I've done my fair share of time at the library. That wasn't my favorite. It was normally only visited by old stuffy people. Most kids my age get all of their information from the internet."

"True," I agree, knowing all too well.

We reach for our glasses of water at the same time, the backs of our hands brushing. She smiles. I return it, lifting the cold water to my mouth while trying to talk myself out of turning it over and dumping it on my head so it can cool me down.

I should've sat across from her instead of right beside her, but who was I to argue with the hostess when she placed our menus on the connecting corner of the table?

"I told you a little about my parents. What about yours? What are they like besides forcing home-cooked meals on you?"

I watch her eyes, and they light up as she waits for me to talk about my own family. She genuinely wants to know. We aren't just sharing small talk while getting through dinner. This is new for me. My normal outings that look similar to this are a rush to eat because both parties already knew how the date was going to end. Hell, many times, the meal was skipped.

A waste of time, as Sophia said to me in my office that first day.

But we aren't wasting time right now, and no matter how badly I want tonight to end like the other dates I've had over the last decade, I know that isn't where this night is going. It can't, and I have to remind myself of that more often than I should.

"My parents are the most loving, supportive people I know. They only live a couple miles from my house, and I see them several times a week. We have dinner together on the weekend when I'm not working."

"So tomorrow?"

"Probably Sunday. They're both retired, and Saturdays are their time away from each other. Mom visits friends, and Dad pretends to know something about golf."

She laughs, twirling her fork in her pasta as she watches my face.

"Tell me about college. I didn't get the leave-home-and-go-crazy experience."

A frown takes over her pretty features.

"I didn't mean anything by it. Sorry, I—"

"No, it's okay." She takes a fortifying breath as she lowers her fork to her plate. "Remember I told you about falling behind in school?"

I nod because I was once again wrong about her work ethic. The woman is a machine in the office. Sometimes, I have to force her out with excuses of checking on a case just to get her to take a breather.

"Last year—" Her jaw snaps shut as her eyes narrow at me. "If you breathe a word about this to my dad, I'll never forgive you."

She points a finger, tapping me in the chest, and I would grin at her intimidation tactic if her face wasn't so serious.

"I'm not friends with your father, Sophia, but even if I was, I wouldn't share your secrets."

No, I'd hold them inside of me so that way I knew more about you than someone else—a treasure I'd appreciate until my last dying breath.

"I had trouble at school last year. A stalker."

I grip the edge of the table, ready to bundle her up, encase her in bubble wrap and drive all the way to Albuquerque without her breathing another single detail. I'd hunt that fucker down and—

"The school handled the situation as best they could, but he stayed right on the side of legal in his creepiness. I was afraid to leave my room, and although I tried to keep up with my schoolwork from inside my dorm, it was just hard with upper level classes, and impossible with the science lab I'd registered for. I had to spend the first half of this semester working through those labs again for credit." She refocuses on her plate, head hung in misery, and I barely keep my finger from crooking under her chin to make her look up at me. "I'm lucky the teacher let me do the labs that way and the dean over the program is letting me shove a full semester of internship into these last couple of months. I would've had to stay another semester."

"You mean you would've had to spend an entire semester following me around?" She lifts her head grinning. "You did get lucky."

"Maybe." Her eyes sparkle, and I have to look away before I mistake the look for something more than it is.

"You didn't tell your dad?" She shakes her head. "Afraid he'd hurt him?"

"I could say my dad would probably kill him then laugh it off as a joke, but I honestly don't know what he'd do to him." I wouldn't blame the man. "I do know what he'd do to me, and I wasn't about to be locked down. I was lucky to go away to college, and it was a subject of contention for a very long time. My senior year of high school was almost ruined by it. I didn't want to be forced to transfer or do online classes from my gilded tower."

"Cerberus is very protective?" I deduce.

"I'm surprised someone hasn't already tracked my phone tonight." She doesn't laugh. "But I'll be even more surprised if we walk outside and there isn't a row of motorcycles waiting to escort me home."

"Seems smothering. Did you let them know where you were?"

"I did. I texted my mom. She told me to have a good time. She's not as strict as my dad despite having grown up in… circumstances."

She gives me a weak smile, and her statement makes me want to dig a little deeper into her life, but I won't do that. Unless I suspect she's in an unsafe situation, I want all of her secrets whispered from her perfect mouth, not discovered from digging into her family's history.

"So no wild parties at school?"

"My freshman year grades were compromised from having a little too much fun, but after I had to retake a math class, I knew I had to calm down. So really just a wild second semester."

"Not a first semester?"

She grins and opens her purse when the waiter drops the check off. I wave her off and pull out my wallet, handing him my card before she can argue. She still pulls a twenty out and drops it on the table.

"For the tip," she explains, and I know there's no sense in arguing. It also won't stop me from tipping the young man myself.

"So, no partying the first semester?" I ask again.

"I was so sheltered growing up. It took that first semester, and my dormmate's incessant begging for me to finally cave and attend a party. After that, I was hooked. I wanted to party every weekend. Thursday night to early Sunday morning you could find me on frat row or at one of the bars playing pool and darts. I was a hellion. Bad things could've happened. Last year was proof of that, but thankfully, I stayed safe."

"Did he hurt you?"

"David?"

"Is that his name? Your stalker?"

She sits back in her seat, and until this moment, I didn't realize just how close we were to each other.

"He didn't hurt me. He texted, called, emailed, slid notes under my door. Gifts were delivered. I didn't return his affections, blew him off once at a party not knowing he was the same guy spamming my school email. I caught him one day trying to slip a package under my door, and I called campus security."

"What was in the package?"

She watches my face, biting the inside of her lip, and it's clear she doesn't want to tell me. I may have to backpedal on the declaration of learning all of her secrets from her own lips.

"A manifesto."

"What?"

"Yeah. So the police said it was like two hundred handwritten pages of his declaration of love and a lot of messed up plans about our future. Until that day I saw him standing outside of my dorm, I wouldn't even have been able to pull him out of a police lineup. He was that unmemorable."

"What happened to him?"

"I didn't read the document he was trying to slide under my door, but it freaked the administration enough to expel him from school."

"Has he contacted you since then?"

Her eyes dart across the room. "He hasn't, but can we talk about something else?"

"Sophia," I reach for her, but she pulls her hand away before I can make contact.

"I should go. Can you give me a ride back to my car?"

"Of course." I stand, pressing my hand against her lower back as we walk out together.

"No motorcycles." She laughs as we step outside, but there's no real humor in her voice.

I open the passenger side of my truck for her but give her space. If she's thinking about that creepy fucker and the liberties he took while pursuing her, the last thing I want to do is make her see some relation between him and me.

I'm mentally berating myself all the way back to the police station parking lot because I wanted tonight to be different, a way to get her mind off the shit day she had, but I failed epically at that.

This is why I don't fucking date.

I can never turn the detective in me off. I want all the facts, all the details, I want to know if she's safe. What that asshole is doing now. Will he come after her again?

She made me promise not to talk to her dad, but fuck, what if she's still in danger? Can he protect her if he doesn't know she needs protecting?

"I had a good time tonight," she says as I pull into the parking lot, lining my truck up beside her car.

"Me too," I tell her, wondering what I can say to get a redo, a chance to make things right before she's gone for the next two days.

Chapter 8

Sophia

I fiddle with my fingers in my lap, making no attempt to get out of his truck. We were in this very situation a couple of hours ago, and once again, it seems like neither one of us want the night to end.

I'm stuck on wondering if this was a date, but he's probably counting down the minutes until my crazy-attracting ass gets out of his truck, all the while regretting asking me to dinner in the first place.

It felt like a date up until I ruined it with my damn stalker story, but the warmth of his hand on my back as we left the restaurant didn't feel like him pulling away.

He opened the truck door for me, waiting for me to put my seatbelt on before closing me inside—gentlemanly things. Things I've seen my dad and the other men in Cerberus do for their women.

Maybe I'm delusional. Maybe I'm like David and only a few more interactions away from writing my own manifesto about my future with Detective Matthews.

I laugh at the possibility.

"Penny for your thoughts?"

"Did you do this on purpose?" I ask, pointing to my car out of the passenger window.

"How do you want me to answer that?"

"Honestly."

"Then yes. It's dark outside, and despite this being city property with probably no less than a half a dozen cops in the near vicinity, crime can still happen."

"It's something my dad would do," I explain with a grin. "Something the guys he works with would do."

"Then I think I like your dad and the Cerberus guys because there's never anything wrong with making sure a pretty girl is safe. Hold tight, and I'll come around."

Without turning the truck off, he climbs out. My eyes follow him all the way around the front of the truck as the headlights reflect off the gun on his hip.

"Do you want me to start it for you?" he asks when he opens up my door.

"I can do it," I tell him, reaching into my purse to grab my key fob.

I crank the car as I climb out of his truck, but for some reason he doesn't take a step back to give me room.

I'm not upset in the least by the fact that he's so close. I was sure I'd ruined the evening and non-date with my horror story, but he's still close.

Not a date.

Not a date.

Not a date.

I chant in my head because it seems I need the constant reminder with him standing right in front of me.

He lifts his hand, pushing back a lock of hair the wind has blown in my face. His hand lingers, his warm palm resting against my cheek.

Before I have the chance to lean into the touch, he clears his throat and takes a step back.

Although I blink up at him, the moment is gone.

I won't press the issue. Today has been too much already, and a rejection from him is just one more thing I'll be forced to stew over for the next two days. Damn if I don't have enough to think about already.

"I'll see you on Monday." I give him a quick smile before stepping around him and climbing into my car.

He stands in the parking lot, staring after me as I pull away, and even though I tell myself I won't, my eyes are locked on the sight of him in the rearview mirror until the night swallows him up.

I can't go home. I'm too raw, too confused about what's going on, feeling too disjointed to see my loving mom and dad sending each other secret looks they think no one else around them can see.

So I don't go home. I head straight to the gas station on the corner and grab a six-pack of tiny wines. Classy as hell I know, but honestly, if no one is around to see you moping with gas station wine, then did it even really happen?

On my way back through town, I drive by the police station, a sinking feeling in my gut when I see his truck is no longer there. Maybe I had it in my head to follow him home, but I spent an hour tonight regurgitating my story about someone creeping on me so it doesn't seem like the best idea. Plus, he's a great detective and would probably spot me before he got out of the damn parking lot.

With that plan thankfully foiled, I head to the park instead. It's dark, so it should be deserted but even if it's not, I anticipate late-night teens up to no good scattering like roaches when my headlights pull into the parking lot.

I don't think about tomorrow when I park my car. I don't worry about what Monday is going to look like, not only the work but the awkwardness that's sure to be there when I have to see Colton again.

I worry about nothing other than finding the perfect playlist on my phone—locking my doors because safety—and twisting off the top of my blush wine.

The first bottle goes down cold, the aftertaste washed away by the second. By the third, I'm bouncing my head to the music, drumming my fingers on the steering wheel as if I joined the band myself. When I twist the top off the fifth one, I can't remember drinking the fourth one, but I'm committed. Exhaustion fills my bones as I sip the sixth, and my eyes won't seem to stay open enough for me to finish it.

My phone dings, the sound echoing around me due to being connect through my car's Bluetooth.

I frown down at the message, but my fingers work quickly with the lie to my dad about staying at a friend's house tonight. I should ask him to come get me, but I don't.

Judgment from him is the very last thing I need tonight. I need a fluffy blanket, a pillow, and warm strong hands all over my body.

Colton's face flashes in my mind of course, but that's a ship that's never going to sail. Nope, that boat is stuck in the slip, dry docked from drought along with my underused pu—

My phone chimes again, and I'm hit with a rush of guilt with my dad wishing me a good night. I groan. I shouldn't have to lie. I don't actually have to lie, and I don't know why I did.

I fire off a text because I have to let someone know where I am.

If I go missing, it's because I have to sleep in my car at the park. I'm not going to risk killing a family of three.

The text goes unanswered, but I'm not surprised. There's no reason for him to respond. Colton has already had to deal with me for like fifty hours this week. I shouldn't be bothering him on his weekend off, anyway. We're not friends. He's sort of my boss.

I could text Griffin, Lawson, or even Cannon. There's no shortage of people I could reach out to at eleven on a Friday night. There's a good chance not a single person I know is already in bed, but my arms are heavy, much like my eyes. Even my soul seems burdened by the week and sleeping right here won't be all that bad. Yeah, I know I'll probably have to mainline Aleve in the morning, and I'll certainly have to explain to my parents why I'm coming home in my work clothes, but I can deal with all of that in the morn—

I squeal like I've just spotted Jason Voorhees with a knife when someone knocks on my window. I cringe away and lift a hand when a megawatt light is shined right in my eyes.

"Open the door," the criminal snaps after trying the handle and getting nowhere. "Sophia, open the damn door."

I know I read somewhere that most people are murdered by people they know, and I have a choice to make. Put the car in drive and risk killing someone, or take the chance with a murderer.

My hand reaches for the gearshift, but then the image of that four-year-old little boy from the drunk driving case sneaks back into memory. I crack the window instead.

"May I help you?"

A husky chuckle fills my ears, and I inwardly wonder if Ted Bundy had such a sexy laugh. If he did, then I completely understand why women jumped at the chance to spend a little time with him.

I smack my forehead with my palm, groaning in pain with the contact. What a fucked up thing to joke about even mentally. The man was a sex offender and serial killer. I once again blame television, and more specifically, Zac Efron for making crazy look so damn appealing.

"Are you drunk?"

"Buzzed," I argue, squinting my eyes but still unable to see well, even though the light is no longer pointed directly at my face. "Too intoxicated to drive."

My phone rings, but I decline the call from Izzy, too invested in the conversation with this stranger to whine to my best friend about Colton fucking Matthews.

"Should I take you to the station?" he asks as he reaches inside the car to hit the door unlock button.

"Fire station?" I muse. "Firefighters are hot."

I snort, an unladylike sound, but the alcohol swimming in my bloodstream tells me it was a cute sound.

The guy chuckles as he opens the door. "And here I thought you had a thing for cops."

I take his hand when he offers it to me, and damn if my eyes are broken because here stands Colton Matthews. Think of the devil and he shall appear.

"I'm not the devil, Sophia." I roll my lips between my teeth because I had no idea I said that last part out loud. Hold on. How much have I said out loud?

"I'm guessing nearly everything you think you thought since I arrived. And if you're taking notes, I think Mark Harmon played a much better Ted than Zac Efron."

"And the sexy laugh part?" I ask, hoping against hope I didn't say that out loud.

"The part about Bundy having a sexy laugh or the fact that you think I have a sexy laugh?"

Kill me now.

"No can do. I work homicide, and I'm off this weekend, remember? Conflict of interest. Let me grab your things and I can see about getting you home."

"I can't go home. I lied to my dad about staying at a friend's house," I explain in a rush as Colton leans me against the car so he can turn off my car and grab my personal belongings. "And I can't leave my car here. It'll end up on blocks."

"We'll drop your keys off at the station so one of the guys can swing by and grab it."

"You're impounding my car?" I scoff, the jerk of my head overexaggerated. "For drinking in my car? Seems a little harsh, don't you think?"

He stands to look at me, his hands full of my belongings. "You are so fucking cute."

I blow a strand of hair from out of my face, but he doesn't take the hint to push it behind my ear. I mean I know his hands are full, but he's missing out on a pretty intense kiss. If he'd only get a couple inches closer, I could seal the damn deal.

"I have no doubt the kiss would be intense, Sophia." He leans in close enough that I can feel his warm minty breath on my lips. "But I don't kiss drunk girls."

"Let's make a deal?" I bargain. "How about when I say stuff out loud, and it's clear I meant to think them, why don't you be a gentleman and keep your mouth shut?"

"Deal," he agrees. "Now get in my truck."

He's so damn bossy. It makes me wonder how bossy he would be in bed. Like would he smack my ass to get my attention or maybe wrap his sexy fingers around my throat?

"Jesus, Soph. Just get in the damn truck." He groans when I look over my shoulder at him.

"Did I—"

"Just get in the damn truck."

Chapter 9

Colton

She's asleep before I can even get back in my truck after securing her car. She doesn't stir when I call one of the guys at the station to grab her car from the park, or when we swing by the station to drop off her keys.

She's snoring softly at the last red light in town, and sawing logs by the time I pull up in my driveway.

Taking her home will be something I already regret, but some of the things in my past I initially saw as a mistake have turned into some of the best things about my life. I'm crossing my fingers that tonight will end up being one of those things as well.

"No regrets," I mutter to myself as I climb out of my truck and walk around to open the passenger side door.

She jolts when I scoop her up in my arms, but she settles back into my embrace quickly. The flowery scent of her skin was once something I looked forward to, but it's a whole other story this close. Especially after realizing as I walk her inside my house that it's concentrated more on the spot under her ear than near her shoulder. I now crave the ambrosia covering her skin. God, what this woman is doing to me.

The lights in the house are still on. I was moments from heading to bed when I got her text, but hadn't made it as far as turning the television off and shutting everything down. I contemplate letting her sleep on the couch, but that's not something I'm going to want to explain in the morning, so like a fool, I carry her to my own damn bed.

I make excuses in my head as I carry her down the hallway, but the simple truth is, I want her in my bed. I want the scent of her skin on my sheets. I want to close my eyes tonight with thoughts of her in my space, the intimacy of it will live inside my brain for eternity.

"I wanted to kiss you," she whispers, her eyes still closed when I settle her on the mattress.

"I know, baby." God, I want that, too.

I grind my back teeth together. She's supposed to be speaking her truths out loud, not me.

"Where am I?" Her words are soft, filled with sleepiness, and she probably won't remember them in the morning. I can only pray she doesn't wake up with regret for calling me.

"You're at my house, Sophia. I'm going to leave the bathroom light on in case you need to get up. I'm going to lock the bedroom door from the inside, so you'll have to call out for me if you need me."

"Thank y—"

She doesn't even get the second word out completely before her body relaxes entirely into my sheets. I tug the comforter up around her shoulders after tugging off her boots. I don't remove another stitch of clothing. I tuck her sock-covered feet under the blanket and leave the room, locking her inside like I promised.

Grabbing blankets and a spare pillow out of the hall closet, I head back to the living room, turning out lights and checking locks on the way.

This isn't even close to how I pictured my night going, and I'm glad I was too lazy to get off the couch and grab the bottle of whiskey I had been salivating over after getting home from eating dinner. I mean, I would've found a way to get to Sophia safely, but I'm just glad I was able to manage it without witnesses. The gossip at a police station is worse than the nurse's station at a hospital, and that's saying something. Those hens cackle incessantly.

I spend the first ten minutes on the couch regretting my decision to purchase a sectional that curves because sleeping in a u-shape isn't fun. After conceding to a crick in my neck in the recliner, I watch the hallway, waiting to see if she's going to need me.

I only saw a six-pack of mini wine bottles, of which I disposed of in the park trash, but that doesn't mean she didn't drink more and discard the empty containers before I got there. I seethe at the idea of her being alone in that park. The crime rate isn't high in that area, but anything could happen at any time.

Resisting the urge to curl up outside the bedroom door, I let my eyes close, but my senses are on full alert. I locked the door so she'll feel safe, but my heart pounds with thoughts of her needing me and not being able to get to her.

I tell myself that she's a grown woman, not a sick child, but it doesn't do much to calm the irrational fear. My fingers are tapping on my chest in arrhythmic anxiety, but I hold steady.

Would she freak if I jimmied the lock open and slept in the bed beside her?

If I did that, would I be able to keep to the far side of the bed, or would I wake up with my arms wrapped around her?

I know the answer to that question no matter how much I want to deny the truth. It's nearly impossible to keep from touching her during the daylight hours when we're awake. Keeping my distance while sleeping wouldn't happen. With the rising sun, I'd have her cocooned in my arms.

I roll my head on my shoulders with the image I've conjured of her soft breath ghosting over my bare chest. Because, of course, I'd only be wearing a pair of boxers.

Jesus, I have to stop.

Shaking my head, I open my eyes, but staring at the sliver of light between the front curtains from the streetlight outside doesn't deter my focus.

When the dog from down the street starts barking, I'm out of the recliner with my nose to the window's glass. The noise gives me an excuse to move, but my reasoning isn't sane. That dog barks every night at the same time when his owner comes home from his second-shift job. I could set my watch by it, but tonight things seem different. Sophia is in my home, intoxicated and vulnerable, and my sense of protection is at an all-time high.

After the dog settles, I slowly make my way down the hall. My ear to the door allows me to hear the soft snores coming from inside, but instead of backing away, I let a smile take over my face as I stand and listen for several long minutes.

"This is stupid," I mutter, but it takes another minute before I pull my face away and head back into the living room.

With determination, I flop back down in the recliner, pull the thin blanket up to my chin, and close my eyes.

I helped a friend out this evening and nothing more. I would've done the same for nearly everyone down at the station had they needed help. Granted, I probably wouldn't have brought them home, but she was adamant about not letting her dad know what was going on. I now know that's because she doesn't want to disappoint him, not out of fear. I don't have a daughter, but I can't say that I'd do things much differently if I did. Dominic was given this precious gift, and he's spent his life protecting it. I've only known her for a few weeks and I have this incessant urge to behave exactly the same way.

Maybe tomorrow will be different. Maybe tomorrow I'll be able to take a long look in the mirror and be able to convince myself that worrying about Sophia isn't my place. She has men in her life—namely her father, uncle, and probably every other man at the Cerberus clubhouse—that are looking out for her.

I just have to make it until the sun rises, and the day will look completely different. Things always seem dire in the middle of the night.

With my eyes squeezed shut, I start the backward countdown from a thousand.

Only it takes me doing it four times before I'm finally able to fall asleep.

Chapter 10

Sophia

The mild headache I wake with is a better outcome than I deserve.

The scent of Colton under my head is a reward I didn't earn with truthfulness.

It doesn't stop me from burying my head deeper to take the spiciness of his cologne into my lungs, but hey, I've always been a little selfish. Admitting you have a problem is the first step, right?

And my problem is Detective Colton Matthews. What started as a little harmless flirtation that first day has somehow morphed into a longing that has taken over nearly every waking thought, and although many of those thoughts—like the ones I'm having now—lean toward the sexual side of things, I also think about everyday things, like drinking coffee together or watching the sun rise. More than once, I've let myself envision what he would look like cooking a meal or doing yardwork.

I punch the pillow under my head, because I know none of that stuff can happen. Dating a man thirteen years older than me? Never going to happen, especially not after acting so irresponsibly last night. What grown man wants to be responsible for a woman who gets drunk in her car at the park?

My intention last night was to just get a break from everything going on, including Colton. I didn't park my car with the hopes that I would end up in his bed. Yet, here I am. I'm moments away from having to do the walk of shame when I haven't reaped any of the rewards. There's no beard-burn marking my skin. My muscles don't ache from overuse.

All I have is a worsening headache and shame.

In an attempt to prolong the inevitable, I regretfully climb out of his bed. I hate the sight of unruffled sheets on the far side. Although I hoped he'd climb in bed with me, I never expected him to. And hope, like most often, is fruitless.

The bathroom is inviting when I step inside, and without a second thought, I strip down and climb in the shower, moaning with relief when the hot water pounds on my back. Tension I didn't know I was holding onto leaves my muscles slowly, and the water is running cold by the time I turn it off.

His towels are soft, something I'd never expect from a bachelor, and I take my time drying off, pausing periodically to breathe in the scent of my skin that is now coated with his fragrance from his body wash. Putting on my clothes from yesterday isn't going to happen. Just the sight of them piled on the floor makes me think about the horror of responding to the scene where a young woman was found dead.

Honestly, I'm no longer thinking about escape, not after spending more time in his space. If anything, I never want to leave. I push down thoughts of consequences and open Colton's closet door, selecting a dark button-down shirt before grabbing the top pair of boxers from his drawer.

I feel like a temptress as I roll the boxers up so they stay on my hips and can't help biting my lip when I take a look at myself in the bathroom mirror. After rinsing my mouth with mouthwash, I gather as much courage as I can muster and leave the room.

I won't do any kind of begging with Colton, but maybe voicing my thoughts to him would help. Maybe if he knew how I felt, things would be different. Maybe if I let him catch me watching him, he would understand how much I desire him. There's only one way to find out, and I'm determined to leave this house today with every one of my cards on the table. Rejection would suck, but at least I can go home knowing how he wants to proceed.

I mastered the art of sneaking around by the time I was twelve, not that I ever got past my dad without him knowing, so I traverse the hallway on the tips of my toes. Pausing just inside of the tidy living room, I take a moment to watch Colton. Asleep in the recliner, he looks incredibly uncomfortable. Having sunk down during the night, his long legs extend past the end of the chair, bare feet hanging out of the end of the blanket.

Guilt swims in my gut. The man worked hard this week, and my antics have relegated him to a horrible night of sleep. I could spend all day watching him, trying to ignore the urge to wake him up with a kiss and insist he go climb in his bed while I make him breakfast, but a noise in the other room distracts me.

Tilting my head, I wait for the noise again, thinking maybe he has a dog or something, but silence surrounds me. Curiosity gets the better of me, my heart pounding with the unknown as I turn in the direction of the sound I heard. I don't find a hungry puppy sniffing around looking for breakfast, but the sight before me does make me pause.

Vibrating back muscles disappear into a pair of low-slung jeans as the man in the kitchen dances to a song playing through a pair of Bluetooth headphones. I don't make apologies and back away and maybe looking back later, I can still use the excuse that my brain is muddled by alcohol. Instead, I stand there and watch, an impressed smile on my lips. This man is tall, the hint of a shadow on his jaw when he turns slightly to grab something from the cabinet.

He's attractive. I'll give him that, but he's got nothing on the man in the other room.

Is he a roommate? Colton didn't offer up much about his homelife, and he seemed reluctant to answer the questions I had about his family last night.

The man turns around, startling for a brief second before a wide smile spreads across his handsome face. Mischievous eyes skate up and down my body from my bare legs to the top of my messy head. He nods in appreciation, and I easily determine he's related to Colton. Not only are the facial features strikingly similar, but he's behaving exactly the same way Colton did when he first saw me. He pulls his headphones from his ears as the flirtatious look on his face grows.

"Good morning."

He's definitely a younger brother, possibly a cousin.

"Morning." Nerves force me to shift from one foot to the other as I weigh the benefits of using this guy to make Colton jealous. Nothing forces a man's hand like competition, but Colton doesn't really seem like the type of man who's willing to fight over a woman.

"I didn't know we had an overnight guest." His eyes continue to rove over the length of me, and I can tell when he notices the pucker of my nipples.

The guy is good-looking, but I'm not aroused by the sight of him. If anything, it's the proximity of the man in the living room that's got my blood heated this morning, but I don't make a move to cover my chest. I'm not indecent. He can't really see anything due to the dark nature of the shirt I chose, but it doesn't stop the man from getting his fill.

"Is there coffee?"

He clears his throat, eyes snapping to mine instead of remaining on my chest.

"Y-yeah, let me get you a cup," he stammers, which is adorable, as he reaches into the cabinet. I don't bother hiding a smile at the sight of his back muscles flexing.

I'm not desperate for attention, but I also won't deny feeling like a queen when I feel his eyes follow me across the room. He steps away so I can pour a cup of coffee, and I know if I look over my shoulder, I'm going to find him still watching me.

Only when I look, teeth digging into my bottom lip because of the power I feel it gives me, I find Colton leaning against the doorframe with his arms crossed over his chest, a messy head of hair, and his sexy mouth in a playful smirk.

"What's going on in here?" he asks before I can muster up an explanation.

"Dad!" the other man yelps. "You scared the shit out of me!"

My eyes widen as they sweep between the two. "D-dad?"

Not a chance.

Nope.

No way.

I attempt to swallow the lump in my throat, but it doesn't budge.

Instead of answering, Colton's eyes sweep down my legs, and I feel like a pervert knowing it looks like I'm not wearing anything under his shirt. Hell, embarrassment heats my cheeks at having the audacity to wear his clothes at all.

When his eyes make it up to my chest, my breasts betray me by growing heavy, nipples furling even more than they were in the cool room. With shaking hands, I grasp the fabric and pull it away from my skin.

"I thought he was your brother. You have a son?" I look over at the young man, who now that I think about it looks younger than he did at first sight. I feel gross.

The guy stares at me, his eyes now staying on my face instead of drinking me in like he was before Colton appeared. I want to shift on my feet. No, I want to run away, but I'm not ten, and I know the problem won't disappear when I leave the room.

"No way," I argue, pausing for them to start laughing and let me in on the joke. "You're too young."

The kid swallows, but it's clear he's deferring the conversation to Colton.

"Rick, why don't you take the trash cans down," Colton instructs, his eyes never leaving mine.

"The trash doesn't run until Monday," Rick argues.

"Now, Rick."

The kid grumbles under his breath, but he disappears, the front door opening and closing less than a minute later.

"I swear to God, I thought he was your brother." My throat is thick with emotions I don't have the time to analyze, and the backs of my eyes burn with unshed tears.

"And that would make you coming out here half-naked okay?"

"I have on your boxers," I assure him, pulling up the hem of the shirt so he can see I'm telling the truth.

His eyes flare, a sharp intake of breath whistling from his nose. He pushes away from the doorframe, inching closer, and it forces me to take a step back.

"I feel like a pervert," I admit.

"He's seen more on Netflix," Colton whispers, his eyes still on my legs. I drop the shirt, letting the fabric kiss the tops of my thighs. "He's not some protected baby."

"I'm s-sorry," I stammer, blinking with shame when his eyes meet mine.

"He's a lucky boy," he continues as he draws closer.

My butt is now against the counter, and even though he's still several feet away, I feel like a caged animal.

"I would've given a year's worth of allowance at his age to walk into the kitchen and find you grinning at me."

My fingers tangle in the fabric of the shirt, nervousness winning out over anything else. Is this where he throws me out? Tells me he never wants to see me again because I was creeping on his teenage son.

"He looks older," I justify. "He has a beard."

"He has stubble because he hasn't shaved in a month." Colton lifts his hand to his own chin. "He hit puberty earlier than most. He had a mustache at thirteen."

"His name is Rick?" I ask, not knowing what else to say.

"Yes."

"Mother?" I look around the kitchen, noticing the lived-in feel of the space. The curtains have lemons on them, and there's a spoon rest on the stove for shit's sake. Tears threaten to fall. "Does she live here? Are you still with her?"

This isn't a bachelor pad. Men don't have seat cushions on dining room chairs, do they?

"I'm not a home-wrecker," I whisper, the very first tear falling from my eye.

No wonder he stopped the flirting that very first day.

God, dinner last night? I let myself believe it was a damn date.

Jesus, what's wrong with me?

Me?

What about him?

I stand to my full height, my false bravery betrayed by the fingers still twisting in the shirt.

Oh God, *his shirt*.

"I'm not married," he says, his body now mere inches from mine. "Only Rick and I live here."

"Where's his mother?"

He shrugs but doesn't offer up any more information.

"How old is he?"

"Sixteen." My brow scrunches together, and he must see that I'm trying to do the math in my head. "Conceived at eighteen, born at nineteen. We were twenty when she decided she no longer wanted to be a mother or a wife."

This is the divorce he mentioned. My heart cracks for him as a man, but splits wide open for their son to not have a mother.

"How did I not know you were a single dad?"

He licks his lips, and it leaves me distracted.

"You are single, right?"

"Can you put the shirt down, Sophia? It's a little distracting."

I gasp when I look down to not only find my fingers tangled in the shirt but also that they're only about an inch or so away from his crotch.

"Shit," I hiss and release the shirt.

His chuckle washes over me, but I nearly stop breathing when I look up and see the heat burning in his eyes.

Chapter 11

Colton

Did she even realize her fingers brushed the front of my jeans?

I didn't miss it. The split-second touch has my blood singing in my veins, but she looks like she's about to cry.

I want to wipe away the single tear that's rolling down her cheek but that would be a mistake.

Bringing her here was a mistake.

Having her in my home is a mistake because I'm seconds away from scooping her up and carrying her back to my bedroom.

"You didn't tell me about him," she whispers, her head hanging down, denying me the sight of her gorgeous brown eyes.

"I'm surprised he hasn't been by the station since you started your internship."

The conversation is casual when I'm feeling anything but inside. Rick stayed with a friend last night, and I didn't expect him home so early.

"I didn't know he was so young." Finally, her eyes lift to mine, shrouded with unease. "I thought he was your brother."

"Were you trying to make me jealous?"

The prospect of it makes me thicken further with possession.

"I thought about it."

"That's not very nice, Sophia. Jealous men seldomly act with reason."

I'm not in competition with my teenage son in the least, but a sick sense of ownership fills me when she bites her lip without answering.

"Almost kissing me and backing away isn't very nice either."

Is she talking about last night or now? Because the urge took over my body in both instances.

"You want to be kissed?"

Her eyes dart away when she refuses to answer.

"Look at me."

She hesitates, taking several long breaths before turning her face toward me.

"I shouldn't want to kiss you," I whisper.

"But you do?"

My tongue wets my lips.

Fuck yeah, I do. "I can't."

"But you want to?"

Kissing her would make so many fantasies come true. My lips on hers, finally knowing what her tongue felt like against mine, is what my dreams have been made of for weeks. Could we cross that line and come out the other end unscathed? My guess is no.

"I can't," I repeat.

"Why not?" She looks so innocent, reminding me of just why I've backed off the countless times I've wanted to be this close to her.

I'm thirty-five with a teenage son. My baggage has baggage. She has her whole life ahead of her. The weight on my shoulders has no business getting close to her. It would be such a disservice to be that selfish.

"It's just a kiss," she barters. "Just one little—"

"No, Sophia. It wouldn't be just a kiss."

Her breath hitches, her eyes wide and blinking.

Can't she understand that one kiss would turn into two and then three? Seconds would tick by and the sun would set tonight with her in my bed and in my arms. Surely she can understand that my lips on hers would only be the beginning of a train wreck both of us would be powerless to stop?

"I want all of that," she says, as if she's capable of reading my mind.

There are parts of me that beg me to change my mind, mostly the areas below my neck, and I falter when I realize the muscle pounding behind my ribcage has somehow gotten involved.

When did things shift from just wanting to be inside of her to wanting to stand beside her, to wanting to be a part of her life in and out of the bedroom?

It's this realization that forces me to take a step, the foot now between us seeming like a wide chasm of indecision.

I don't know that walking away from her is possible, but I have to try. We're in totally different places in life, and I come with a nearly grown child.

I don't know what it is about her that makes the entire situation different. I've been with women since Rick's mother left, but not one of them tempted me the way she does. Not one of those women made me pause and want to think about the future.

It's not because she's beautiful, I've known beautiful women before.

Is it because the age difference is a little taboo? Maybe because she's off-limits according to the unspoken decree set out by her father's club? Because we work together and that means I should keep my distance?

Even with knowing all of that, do I *have* to stay away?

A rush of breath leaves my lips as she watches me.

Yes, I do, because I've got intentions of trapping her in a life with me, and just sex won't work. Just one kiss isn't possible. One of anything with her would just be a fool's errand.

"Sophia, I think—"

"Is it because of how I acted with Rick? I swear I—"

"I'm not mad about that," I assure her, my feet itching to step near her again.

I'm obsessed with her lips, the soft pillows twitching as I watch them. My cock is full and throbbing, and that's the power this woman has over me. One look, one hint of her mouth on mine and I'm ready to bury myself inside of her.

"But you are mad?"

Fucking furious. Exceedingly irritated at the compromises I'm making in my head.

"You've done nothing wrong, but this needs to—"

"Dad, look who came for a visit."

I don't even have to turn around to look when Rick talks. There are only two people in the world who come in this house aside from Rick's friends.

"Fuck," I mutter, willing my heavy cock to deflate.

"Colton?"

Yep, that's about all it takes. Slowly, I turn around, giving my parents a weak smile, hoping they can't see the agitation at being interrupted even though it couldn't have come at a better time.

I block their view of Sophia, not because I'm ashamed of her being in my home, but to save her the unease of meeting them while half-dressed.

"Mom. Dad. How lovely to see you this morning."

Mom cocks an eyebrow. Dad huffs a laugh, and for the first time in my life I feel like a teenage boy getting caught doing something wrong.

And that's saying something because I had to confess to them that I was going to be a father four months before high school graduation.

Chapter 12

Sophia

Parents?

Parents!

Only me. I swear, if there is something else that could go wrong today, it will.

I'm in Colton's button-down shirt, a pair of his rolled up boxers, and it looks like we're having a fucking family reunion in the kitchen. I haven't even had coffee yet, and I've managed to sort of flirt with his teenage son—cringe—and get caught by the man's parents half-naked.

If this were some late-night sitcom, I'd squeal like a trapped pig and run away, but as established earlier, the situation doesn't disappear when you leave the room.

Peeking around Colton's massive shoulder, I see his mother, a beautiful woman with his same warm brown eyes, standing with a stoic look on her face. His dad, on the other hand, is grinning, throwing me a silly wink when I make eye contact with him. Is every man in this family a hopeless flirt?

Rick is leaning against the doorframe looking so much like his dad that I want to gag at the memory of thinking of him in any other way.

Colton turns so he can swipe his gaze back and forth between his parents and me. If there were cheesy music playing in the background, I'd swear I was standing on the set of that television show I thought about earlier.

No one is saying anything, and I don't know if they're just at a loss for words or if they're deferring to me.

What I do know is that I hate the spotlight, and my face is absolutely on fire.

We were seconds away from kissing for the first time. I'm certain of it. I could tell he was debating the merits of it, but the scale was beginning to tip in my favor, and now this!

"Dad's friend stayed the night last night," Rick helpfully offers.

Colton clears his throat, and I'm once again near tears.

"Sophia, these are my parents, Franklin and Sally Matthews. Mom and Dad, meet Sophia Anderson."

I give them a little wave, glued in this spot and unable to offer my hand to shake. They both say good morning, and I don't get the vibe that they think I'm being rude. His dad, thankfully, keeps his eyes on mine. I can't say the same for Rick.

Colton crosses the room and leans over to whisper something in Rick's ear, making the boy turn around and leave the room.

"Mom and Dad, we'll join you in the living room shortly."

They both turn but his mom looks over her shoulder, watching me as she walks away.

"You said they play golf and visit friends on Saturday," I hiss, but Colton holds up his hand to silence me.

"She's gorgeous," I hear his mother whisper. "A little young, but absolutely gorgeous. I need more grandbabies."

I only thought my skin was on fire before. What's hotter than fire? That's where I'm at right now.

Grandbabies?

What. The. Actual. Fuck?

"Do you think she's related to those Anderson bikers?" his father questions before their voices trail off into the other room.

My hackles go up, and it's not lost on me that I'm half-naked in this man's kitchen and have no right to question others' opinions, but my family is a hotspot for me.

It's clear Colton's trying to hide a smile when he turns back around to face me.

"Still want that kiss now?"

I swallow, backing away because my head is swimming with a million and one questions. He gives me an almost imperceptible nod of understanding.

"There are more appropriate clothes waiting for you on my bed." And now I know what he whispered to his son.

I scurry past him, not even looking in the direction of his parents when I run by the living room.

Rick is leaving his dad's room when I try to enter. His eyes trail down my legs once again.

"Not a chance, buddy," I snap before stepping into the room and closing the door.

Much to my horror, Colton's more appropriate clothing includes a pair of sweats and a Farmington High t-shirt. Nothing says I'm too young for him like replicated clothing that I wore only a few years ago.

In no position to argue, I change, leaving his boxers on out of spite. I don't linger in his room because I don't want to appear even more rude than I know I already look. As I make my way down the hall toward the living room, I pray Colton will offer to take me to get my car. My earlier interaction with Rick seems even more skeevy considering what I was wearing. I don't imagine they'll care that I came out first thing this morning thinking Colton and I were alone in the house.

The end of the hallway opens up to the sight of all four Matthews sitting in various places with coffee in their hands. Well, Rick is drinking a glass of milk because he's a fucking child.

My stomach turns as I look around the room. The only spot left to sit is between Colton and Rick, but I don't have the nerves for that right now. Colton pats the spot with an open hand. I eye the front door before looking back at him, and I don't miss the challenging look in his eyes. Does he think I can't handle spending time with his family?

I mean, I don't know that I'll survive it, but I've never been one to back down from a challenge.

I cross the room, a small smile playing on my lips and take a seat. Colton doesn't open his mouth to begin a conversation, and neither does anyone else.

Silence swirls around us, and I see everyone smiling. It's as if I've stepped into the middle of a family joke, and I'm the only one who doesn't know the punchline.

"Would you like a cup of coffee?" Colton whispers low in my ear.

Goosebumps travel down my arm, and the question feels more intimate than it should with three other people in the room.

"I'm fine," I assure him, but he doesn't inch back, doesn't put distance between us.

A drop of sweat forms between my shoulder blades, trickling down my spine.

"How do you know our son?" his dad asks, and everyone in the room seems invested in my answer.

"We met at the police station." His mom tilts her head, and I realize I haven't offered enough information. I can't tell if she thinks he arrested me or something. "I'm working an internship there."

"You're still in college?" Mrs. Matthews asks.

I answer her honestly, trying not to give too much information while at the same time attempting not to seem evasive.

Colton doesn't offer anything up, and why should he? They aren't interrogating him. I'm the one under the spotlight. Rick eventually wanders off, but I'm stuck in the living room answering a million questions. They don't ask relationship questions but rather only personal questions, starting with school and family before ending with goals. By the time they stand to leave, I feel like I've sat through an interview for the damn FBI.

"We would love to have you over tomorrow evening for family dinner," his mom says before they step out onto the front porch.

Looks like I got the job, I think.

I give her a noncommittal answer, but it seems like enough for her as she waves goodbye.

Within minutes of his parents pulling out of the driveway, I'm back in his truck on my way to pick up my car from the police station.

Conversation is limited, as in nonexistent. He asked if I needed a bag for my dirty laundry before we left the house and hasn't said much since. I climbed into the truck while he was getting his wallet just so I wouldn't have to put either of us through the awkwardness of him opening my door for me.

My hand is clutching the door handle as we pull into the parking lot at the station. He parks the same way he did last night after dinner, but in the light of day it feels more like a quicker way to get rid of me.

"Thank you for helping me last night," I mutter before climbing out of the truck.

In my hurry to get away, I leave the bag of clothes in the floorboard of his truck, but I'd rather buy an entirely new wardrobe than go back for them. I don't cry on the way home, and I'm relieved my parents are nowhere to be found as I lock myself in my room.

Monday is going to be the worst, and I'm already thinking of what to say when I call in sick.

Chapter 13

Colton

I'm not well rested. I'm not bright-eyed and ready to get the week started. I don't arrive early, overcome with eagerness to see Sophia.

I drag my sleepy ass into work ten minutes late, exhausted from three nights with limited sleep.

Sophia isn't in my office when I open the door and a pang of loss hits me in the chest, but I don't deserve the right to go look for her. I last half an hour alone in my office before I tell myself I'm emerging to get a cup of coffee. Distracted, I left mine sitting on the counter at home. I fire off a text to Rick to make sure he checks to be sure the pot is turned off before heading to school because I can't remember if I did or not. He texts back with some bullshit about me being a senile old man. I'd normally argue with him, but I'm not feeling it this morning.

It's a blessing that Sophia isn't surrounded by cops this morning when I find her working quietly in the corner. I think I'll lose my shit if I have to witness another blowhard hitting on her.

She doesn't look up at me when I cross the room or when I make more noise than necessary while getting a cup of coffee, and for some reason I walk out of there and back to my office without opening my mouth either.

The day drags by, filled with paperwork and phone calls, absent of Sophia's pretty face, and by lunchtime I'm itching to just talk to her, wishing things could be like they were before dinner Friday night. Things shifted, and I'm not liking the outcome. This is what I expected would happen if I slept with her, knowing she wouldn't be very happy with me when I told her we couldn't be anything more, but I didn't even reap the reward of spending the night with her, and I'm suffering the punishment like I did.

I work through lunch, not wanting to submit anyone else to my surly ass attitude, and it's nearly three in the afternoon before my door swings wide. I open my mouth to yell at the person interrupting me, but it's Sophia walking in with a pile of folders.

"Soph," I say, the one syllable sounding more like a plea than I intended.

She doesn't even look at me as she drops the files on my desk.

"Please," I beg, reaching for her wrist before she can turn and walk away.

She freezes, her eyes glued to the contact on her skin.

I keep my hold on her as I stand and join her on the other side of my desk, only releasing her long enough to close the office door. She's glaring at me when I turn back around.

"Can we talk about it?"

"About what?" I love the way she cocks her hip out to the side, but I don't think she'll find it funny that I think she's cute right now. "I'm working. That's why I'm here, remember?"

"About Saturday morning—"

Before I can apologize, she closes the distance between the two of us, pressing her lips to mine. Shocked, I stand frozen, eyes open and blinking down at her. Her eyes flutter for a brief second, but she pulls back almost immediately.

Being the brave woman I've come to admire, she doesn't look away from me. She doesn't hang her head in embarrassment at my inaction.

"You're too young," I say, clearing my throat when the words sound like a lie even to my own ears. "We have to keep things professional."

"And that's what's wrong with Saturday morning," she hisses through her teeth, that fiery attitude I've only seen a couple of times coming out. "You tell me I'm too young, but you're the one who acted like an adolescent boy in front of your parents. You're the one playing around, and I'm too fucking mature for games."

She sidles around me, flying out of my office without another word. She doesn't slam the door behind her when she leaves, and without that final act, things seem left unfinished.

My cell phone rings before I even have the chance to settle back in my desk and overthink all the ways I've fucked up in the last month. The last thing I need as a distraction is a female murder victim with three bullet holes in her chest and a boyfriend that seems to have fled the scene.

***

"Tell me what you see."

Sophia looks around the small home, taking in every inch of the mess made. I don't miss the fact that her eyes avoid the woman's body crumpled near the entryway to the kitchen.

"Chaos," she answers.

"What else?"

"A man lives here."

"How do you know?"

"There are three pairs of men's shoes near the door. The jacket hanging on the hook is too large for her. There's a pile of men's belongings on the front porch."

"What do you think happened?"

"She tried to kick him out. He wasn't happy, and he killed her."

"The boyfriend's name is Dennis Milton," Ramshaw says as he joins us in the room.

His eyes are on the notebook in his hands. Mine are on Sophia.

"Penny was on the phone with 911 when she was shot. She was deceased by the time officers made it to the location."

Sophia flinches with the news. Sometimes it only takes minutes for the unthinkable to occur.

"Dispatch heard them arguing. There were four gunshots, only three hitting the victim. One went wide. Peterson found the other bullet lodged in the bottom cabinet in the kitchen."

"He continued to shoot her as she fell," Sophia deduces.

"There's a BOLO out for Milton's late model Ford Ranger," Ramshaw continues. "He left his wallet on the nightstand in the bedroom, so I don't imagine he has much money with him. He's limited on what he can do. A unit has already been sent to his mother's house across town."

"Thank you," I tell Ramshaw who nods at both of us before backing away.

We continue to work the scene, Sophia taking notes and writing down everything I say out loud. I'm grateful I have better control over my thoughts than she did intoxicated on Friday night because I'm awash with thoughts of her and regrets for my actions. This isn't the time or the place to have that conversation.

We stand out of the way as the crime scene guy takes photos of nearly everything in the house. Having too much is always better than not having enough. Within an hour of us being on scene, a call comes in that the unit sent to Milton's mother's house was able to locate him. After a short standoff, Dennis Milton surrendered and is currently in custody on his way to the police station.

Sophia follows me to the car without a word, and I know that her sullenness is from a combination of what happened earlier in the office and knowing that another life is gone all too soon.

Interrogating suspects never gets easier. Facing evil drains me each and every time I'm tasked with doing it. Procedure sates that Sophia, not a licensed peace officer, can't be in the room with us, but Monahan has given her permission to watch on the other side of the two-way glass. She hasn't witnessed this part of the process yet. She's halfway through her internship, and with any luck, she won't have the opportunity again. We've had too many deaths recently, and the entire department is long overdue for a break from it.

I'm nervous as I enter the room, folder in hand and come face-to-face with Dennis Milton for the first time. I've interviewed hundreds of people in my time on the Farmington Police Force, hundreds of times with people in the other room, but my nerves are on edge knowing that she's on the other side of the glass at my back.

She may see things differently after today. She may have preconceived notions from watching television about what it's really like in an interrogation room, but everyone interviews differently. Hell, each interview is different.

I can only hope she'll still respect me when today is done.

Chapter 14

Sophia

Rubbing the outside of my arm, I watch through the glass as Colton enters the interrogation room.

"Hey, Milton."

How is his voice so calm after leaving the crime scene?

"I bet you've had better days."

Milton doesn't look up from the table to engage with him as Colton informs him that the interview is being recorded. He states the guy's name, the date, and the location of the interview. He even mentions that Milton is handcuffed on his right wrist to the table and the brand of handcuffs being used.

"He's one of the best interviewers we have," Chief Monahan says as he joins me in the room. "His tactics are a little strange, just thought I'd warn you."

"Women, am I right?" Colton asks, and my hackles go up.

"She fucking kicked me out, man. I pay goddamn rent on that place. She didn't have any right."

"Legally, that's your place, too," Colton agrees. "I know I'd be pissed if I came home and saw all of my shit sitting on the front porch."

"She did that shit while I was in the garage changing the oil in *her* fucking car."

"Really?" Colton sounds angry by proxy by the way this murderer was treated. "That's pretty fucked up."

"The fucked up part is that chick she was mad about wasn't even worth it, but the bitch wouldn't listen. Bad sex shouldn't fucking count, man. It was one mistake, and she just went apeshit on me."

Milton throws his hands up in disgust, the one handcuffed only moving a few inches. I flinch with the action, but Colton doesn't budge an inch.

"She hit you?" I could choke Colton right now. Blaming the victim? Not on my watch.

"Easy," Monahan says, his hand on my arm, and I realize I took a step closer to the glass. "Just watch."

"Hit me?" Milton scoffs. "The bitch wouldn't dare."

"So you were just pissed when you shot her?"

Milton doesn't backpedal. He doesn't open his mouth and ask for an attorney. He grins. The man fucking grins, and if I didn't know that he was a murderer, I could see how Penny found him attractive. Surely she was able to see the malice in his eyes.

"She called the cops."

"I'm a cop," Colton reminds him.

"You're just doing your job. She knew better. She knows not to get other people involved in our business."

"Now she's dead."

"And I'd kill her again if I had a chance."

"She's fucking dead, man. You killed her."

"I loved her, too."

Misplaced sobs fill the room, and instead of Colton standing and leaving the room, having gotten the confession, he grabs a box of tissue from the side table and slides it in Milton's direction. The man takes a couple, dabbing the tears from his eyes, and I've seen enough.

My phone buzzes in my pocket and since I told myself I was no longer going to work past the parameters of my internship, I let Monahan know I'll be back to the station tomorrow morning and leave.

I give a hundred percent while I'm there, but I can no longer stick around. Colton wants professionalism. He said as much in his office earlier when I tried to kiss him, so professionalism is what he's going to get. That means no more long hours. No more helping after five o'clock. No more dinners with low lighting. No more drunken texts or kitchen confessions. No sleeping at his house or showering in his home. No conversations with his parents or awkward interactions with his son.

I'll come in, work, and leave. We won't see each other in public. I won't watch him from across the room. Hell, I won't even work in his office anymore. The corner in the breakroom is noisy, but I'll make it work. I only have a month left anyway.

I can't face my parents, so I take the turn toward the clubhouse. There's always something going on there, and if not, the indoor pool is always a fun time. When I pull into the parking lot, I see my dad's SUV near the front door, so I turn right back around and leave the property.

I feel raw, like there's an open wound in my chest which I know is crazy. I know it doesn't make sense for Colton's earlier rejection to hit me so hard, but here I am, miserable and wanting to vent.

Izzy has been distant lately, and I know she won't be in the mood to listen to me complain about losing a guy I never even had, so calling her isn't an option. The idea of going back to the station pulls at me, but I resist, wondering how long I'll last before I cave.

I choose the gym instead, needing to release all of my frustrations. The kickboxing class is packed and twenty minutes in when I arrive, so I don't join them. I hate when class is interrupted, and I wouldn't do that to anyone else. The room with all the treadmills is steaming, thick with the perspiration and humid breaths of the after-work crowd. The machine weight room is packed with meatheads chatting about protein powder and the proper weight increase for back day. The free weight room is filled with men and women alike posing in the mirror. The hallway leading back to the treadmill room is housing four teenage girls filming a *Tik Tok*, and as I begrudgingly climb on a treadmill, I'm regretting even coming here to begin with.

I run hard and fast, giving everything I've got, but my mind still wanders. The last month has drained me, and as much as I'd like to mentally blame Colton, I know the numerous crime scenes have also had an impact. Seeing a dead body is one thing, and I honestly think I can handle that part of the job, but it's the backstory, the flimsy reasoning for the loss of a life that is stealing bits and pieces of me.

Dad told me working in this field wasn't going to be a good fit for me, but I dug in my heels. I don't like being told *no* or *you shouldn't do that*. I changed my major to criminal justice from sports medicine after one simple conversation over an episode of *Brooklyn Nine-Nine* of all things. Police work looked fun, and I voiced that opinion. Dad grew more serious than I've ever seen him, reminding me that the real world isn't like what we were watching. Of course, I knew it wasn't, although hilarious, that show is completely ridiculous. But, he told me no, and I wasn't going to let him stop me.

And look at me now, running on a treadmill, so frustrated I feel like crying because bad things are happening to people and there isn't a damn thing I can do about it.

Hot tears mix with the sweat running down my face, and I nearly jump to the ceiling when a hand taps me on the shoulder. I look over without thinking, nearly losing my footing. Cannon wrinkles his brow, pulling the emergency key from the machine.

"Hey. What are you doing here?" I ask stupidly because it's a damn gym. I already know what he's doing here.

With another frown, he pulls the headphones from my ears. "Are you okay?"

I look around the room to find no less than half a dozen people glaring at me like I ruined their night. I let Cannon guide me from the room, and by the grace of God, the teens are no longer dancing at the end of the hall.

"Take this." He offers me a bottle of water, and I chug it.

"Where's Rivet?"

"Working. They left late last night."

"And my dad?"

"With them in South America. Wanna explain why you're trying to kill yourself in there?"

I try to hand him back the half-empty bottle, but he waves it off.

"Bad day at work?"

"Is that the answer or are you asking me?"

"Are you always this annoying?"

"Yes," he deadpans as I unscrew the cap of the water and take another drink. "And you know it. Tell me what's wrong. Boy problems?"

I sputter, spraying water on the commercial grade carpet at our feet. "Definitely not *boy* problems."

"So what then?"

"Any chance you'll just leave it alone?"

He crosses his arms over his chest. "None, now spill."

"Have you ever made a choice in life and realize it was the wrong one?"

"Many times. Every woman before Rivet was a mistake."

I make a gagging noise. "I'm talking about like work or school, not sex."

He winks at me, but there's no sexual vibe to it. The man is madly in love with his woman, and even though I thought I had a crush on him in years' past, there's none of those feelings lingering around at all. If my face wasn't already flushed from running, I know he'd be able to see how embarrassed I am for trying to kiss him that one time.

"I thought I'd be living in Denver after graduation."

"You're not going?"

He graduates next month just like I do, his degree coming from San Diego. He's one of the ones who met the love of his life and changed his path to line up better with hers. This last year of his has been spent doing classes online.

"I'm working for Cerberus, and I don't see that as a step down, more like a step to the left. I'm working in my field of choice, and every night, well most nights, I get to lay my head down beside Rivet's. I'm a happy fucking man."

"That's good." I focus on my hands.

"But it's clear you're doubting your own choices?"

"Clear, huh?" I huff a humorless laugh. "I don't think I can do the criminal justice field. I've seen more dead bodies, dead kids, and people dead inside from loss. I'm just not cut out for it."

I don't mention that I want to stay in Farmington and at the same time keep my distance from Colton, which is impossible because even if I got a job working for the Sheriff's Department instead of the PD, we'll still end up crossing paths.

"Then do something different."

I lift my eyes, glaring at him.

"It's not that simple. I'm a damn month from graduation, Cannon." I drop to the floor, pressing my back against the wall. He follows and takes a seat beside me.

"Maybe it is. Have you considered academia?"

"I don't want to be a teacher."

"Not even college?"

"And follow in Jasmine's footsteps?"

"There's nothing wrong with being a teacher. Cerberus is filled with them. It's a respectable profession."

"It's safe," I argue. "I want to be a badass."

He laughs at this, but it's not in a mocking tone. "If you think I'm going to spew some shit about gender roles, you're mistaken. Rivet kicks ass as some commando chick and I sit behind a desk, but you can always be a badass teacher, someone who changes people's lives. You can make a difference."

"Yeah," I agree, but I know he's given me something to think about.

"Now, get off your lazy ass and let's go lift some weights. You can't be a badass with such skinny arms."

Laughing, I follow him downstairs to the weight room with a little portion of the burden lifted from my shoulders.

Chapter 15

Colton

No matter the amount of conviction I had when I told Sophia we could only be in a professional relationship, I regret every word I uttered that day in my office.

There hasn't been any flirting or secret smiles.

There are no jokes.

There has been no extra time. She arrives within minutes of her responsibilities in the mornings and leaves promptly at five in the evening.

She doesn't look over her shoulder to make sure she's doing something right.

She doesn't sit at my desk and eat lunch.

We don't argue about opinions on television shows, something we always found middle ground on.

Nope, none of that. It's all business, all the time.

I haven't caught her eyes on me or a single salacious look on her pretty face.

I also haven't caught her talking to the patrol officers either, which has been a blessing. If she ignored me and then turned around and handed her attention so readily to others, I'd probably go insane.

Once again it's Friday, the weekend looming over me like a dark cloud. In two weeks, she graduates, and that means she only has eight more days in the office. What happens after that is anyone's guess. That's a lie. What happens is, she walks away and never looks back. She hasn't asked Monahan about the police academy or if there were office jobs available. I know because I asked him. She hasn't mentioned her after-internship plans with me because we hardly talk. If we aren't discussing a crime scene, her lips are closed.

She's polite but distant. She's not rude, but she's no longer the peppy girl that walked into my office six weeks ago either. Some of her light is gone, and I don't know if that's solely because of me or if some of the blame can land at the feet of the cases we've been working.

This week has been brutal, but after working all night, the suspect was arrested, a full confession was gained, and another case is closed. Everyone at the station is exhausted, but there are smiles all the way around. Even Sophia's lips tilt up a little when Monahan congratulates her on the work she's done. She was instrumental in helping to solve the case, noticing a few discrepancies at the scene on Monday and voicing her opinion about them. Her reasoning was wrong, but it helped get me on the right track, and I wouldn't have been able to do that if it wasn't for her.

"So first round on me?" Gaffey asks the room.

Several readily agree, but I already know Sophia's answer. Each time we close a case, I ask her to dinner to celebrate, and each time she turns me down. She doesn't even give me an excuse like she did the first two times. Her simple no is all I get these days.

"No thank you," she says when Gaffey turns his attention to her.

"You sure?"

"I'm sure." Her eyes meet mine for the briefest second before she turns her attention to Monahan. "Do you mind if I cut out of here a little earlier today?"

"Sure thing, kiddo. Thanks for your help this week. Have a great weekend."

My eyes track her across the room, feet nailed to the floor when she enters my office to get her things. With everyone around, I don't even consider following her, but my eyes follow her until she's clear of the building.

"What about you, Matthews?" Gaffey slaps me on the back. "Wanna join us at *Jake's* for a couple beers."

"Naw, man. Not tonight. I still have some shit to wrap up. Have a good time though."

I leave my colleagues in the front office and head back to my own workspace, shuffling shit on my desk until their laughs and congratulations die off. I lied to my fellow detective. I don't have a damn thing to do tonight, or all weekend for that matter. Sophia has spent so much time working and avoiding me that my desk is completely cleared. Other than the cold case I've been working on the last couple of months, I have nothing left to do.

Leaving my office, I turn off the light and head to my truck. Maybe Rick will be around tonight and we can hang out. That idea is ruined before I get to my truck by a text letting me know he's staying with a friend tonight. Maybe a couple beers with the guys from the station isn't such a bad idea.

Knowing we're low on a few things at the house, I swing by the grocery store before heading in that direction. Hell, with Rick occupied, maybe tonight would be a good night to head up to Durango. There's a little bar there that's always proven to be good for picking up a woman. Just the thought of crawling into a bed and losing myself for a couple of hours with someone other than Sophia makes my stomach turn.

Yep, well and truly fucked.

Once inside the grocery store, the task of grabbing a few things feels like more energy than I have to waste, but I skirt around people shopping and indiscriminately shove things in the damn cart. The good thing about teenage boys is that they can make a meal from practically anything so it doesn't really matter what I end up carrying home. Rick will eat it.

"Detective," I hear from behind me, and I cringe before turning around.

It isn't an angry citizen or someone I've arrested in the past. It's worse.

"Mr. Anderson," I say, holding my hand out.

"Dominic, please. This is my wife, Makayla."

I shake her hand as well. I've never met this man before, but I know Kincaid and they look so much alike it's uncanny. I've also looked him up in the system, just to verify a few things, and I've seen his driver's license photo.

"How's work?"

I scan Dominic's eyes, wondering exactly what he's wanting to hear from me. I give him the answer I pray he's looking for.

"Good. Sophia has been such a big help. There are many people in the office who are going to miss her after the end of next week."

"You should come to her graduation party next Saturday," Makayla offers.

"I—"

"Seven in the evening at the clubhouse," she continues.

Would declining be a red flag? A mentor would go to help a student celebrate, right?

"That would be nice. Should I bring a dish?"

"We've got it covered," Dominic answers for his wife.

Silence settles around us, and I grow uncomfortable. Is this what Sophia felt like in front of my parents? If so, shit, I can see why it pissed her off so much.

"She's going to make an amazing detective one day," I say to fill the weirdness surrounding us.

"Thankfully we don't have to worry about that for a few more years," Makayla says, a soft hand on Dominic's chest as she looks up at him.

"Sophia is planning to go to graduate school for her master's degree before deciding on a career path," Dominic explains.

"She mentioned maybe teaching college," Makayla adds.

"She'd make an amazing teacher," I agree.

"Well, we better get going. See you at the clubhouse Saturday after next."

I raise my hand for a little wave, and despite feeling like I handled myself well, I can see in Dominic's eyes that I'm not fooling him. He knows something is off where Sophia and I are concerned. I hover around the produce section, watching and waiting for them to leave before deserting my shopping cart and getting out of there.

The bar and a few drinks with the guys is sounding like a great idea right about now. Sitting at home thinking about a girl that doesn't want to be thought about is ridiculous.

Knowing how my night is going to end up, I drive home, park my truck, and order an Uber to *Jake's*. I'll be in no condition to drive once I'm done trying to drink her out of my mind.

Once I step inside *Jake's*, my eyes automatically dart to the tables in the far corner. I clock at least five guys I know are linked to Cerberus, and wouldn't doubt if there were more on the dance floor, but I don't see Sophia with them.

Gaffey yells my name from the other side of the bar, holding up a beer in one hand and an empty shot glass in the other.

"Glad you could make it!" He slaps my back when I approach. "Grab a shot."

I pick one up from the table, tossing it back without asking what it is first. Rookie mistake.

"Fuck," I sputter, lifting the back of my hand to my mouth in a failed attempt to stave off the burn.

"Everclear," Gaffey hisses on a laugh. "No sense in wasting time tonight."

Haden is a good guy, but sometimes the job makes life nearly impossible to live without kicking back every once in a while. I don't see his wife around, but if he's here, she can't be far.

A waitress brings another round of beers and shots for the table, and I don't waste time drinking them down. I'm smiling at a couple dancing to the side when I start on my third round, knowing I'm going to be the dad that will end up calling my child tonight for a drunken ride home. I don't think Rick will mind even though he's staying at a friend's house. Hell, he used the running errands excuse for reasoning when he begged for his own vehicle. I don't think the hand-me-down Ford 150 was what he had his sights on, but the kid never complained.

"Hey!" I grin, looking over at one of the newer patrol officers that joined us. "How?"

"Excuse me?" I ask, nearly screaming over the loud music.

I move around Gaffey who has found his wife and slide in next to the guy trying to get my attention. Like all friendly drunks in a bar, he slings his arm around my shoulder like we're best friends. I don't even know this guy's name, but I go with it because I haven't thought about Sophia in at least half an hour.

Well, I guess I just fucked that streak up.

"What?" I ask again when he settles against me.

"How can you spend five days a week around that hot piece of ass and not spend half the day fucking her over your desk?"

I take a step back, letting his arm fall away from me. I could punch this guy in the mouth for saying shit like that. The protective part of me wants to lay his ass out. The drunk part of me wants to tell him it's been hell to spend time with her. I don't do either of those things, opting to just glare at him instead.

"I mean, look!"

I follow the point of his finger and fucking sure enough, there's Sophia. She's not dressed for the bar. She's in her work clothes just like everyone else at our table. Twenty feet away, she's smiling and laughing while playing darts with Ramshaw.

A hand that's moments away from sporting five broken fingers rests on her hip as she tosses the dart at the board, laughing when she misses the thing completely. Ramshaw, being the laid back decent guy that I know he is, doesn't seem irritated that his partner is going to make them lose the game. Of course he's not. He's as fucking charmed by her as every other person in the damn office, myself included.

My mind wanders back to the time she confessed about thinking of making me jealous in my kitchen, and I know this isn't one of those times. I don't catch her looking at me once as I stand there and stare holes in the back of her head. Another ten minutes go by without her looking around at all. There's a good chance she doesn't even know that I'm here being tortured just by her presence and the distance between us.

Leaning in close to Ramshaw's ear, she tells him something before walking toward the back of the bar. He watches her walk away, and hell, so do I.

I can't believe she's here after turning down the offer to come at the office. Did she do it because she didn't want to be near me? Did she simply get bored and change her mind?

I need answers to these questions, and it seems Ramshaw has thought of a few things he needs to tell her too because he's making his way across the bar toward the restrooms as well.

Not on my fucking watch.

"Nope," I tell him with a hand against his chest when he tries to walk by.

"I need to piss," he snaps.

"You can wait until she comes out or you can piss outside."

His eyes dart between mine but decides against arguing. I know he was planning to corner her in the hallway. I don't think he has ill intentions with Sophia, but kisses are easily stolen in private. I'll be damned if he's going to get something that belongs to me.

Chapter 16

Sophia

Cold water from the faucet doesn't take the edge off the trembling in my hands, and I don't think anything will. Ignoring Colton at the station isn't easy, but it's manageable since I can leave his office and work in the breakroom. Ignoring him after realizing he's here at *Jake's* was nearly impossible even with Dillon's distracting game of darts. I'm an excellent dart player, largely in part because I grew up around a bunch of bikers with a dart board on the wall of the clubhouse. You wouldn't know that from watching me play tonight, though.

I blame Colton. Hell, I blame Colton for nearly everything these days.

Bad hair day? Colton.

The flat tire I had on the way to work Tuesday? Colton.

The new dart holes in the wall tonight? Colton.

Everything is his fault, even the flush in my cheeks, heavy breathing, and the knot in my stomach each time I think about walking out of this bar tonight and not cutting my eyes in his direction.

The distance I've put between us the last couple of weeks has been harder than I ever anticipated, and my resolve is breaking quickly.

I watch my eyes in the restroom mirror, knowing that dark circles are hidden under a layer of makeup. I've seriously wondered if I'm losing my mind because it doesn't make sense. I've had crushes before. I've been attracted to guys at school that turned me down or didn't show any interest. I'm not new to rejection, although it doesn't happen very often. That's more on college guys' lack of being very selective, but pressing my mouth to Colton's only for him to look down at me like I violated him hit harder than I ever thought it could.

Arguments in my head are a constant whisper.

If the man doesn't want you, Sophia, move on.

It's that simple.

But I'm finding that it isn't simple at all.

I growl in frustration, turning the tap off and drying my hands.

So what that he's here, probably less than a hundred feet away? I've been coming to this bar for years, long before I was legally able to belly up to the bar. He doesn't own the space, and I shouldn't let his presence deter my evening.

With a straightened spine and head held high, I walk out of the restroom, ready to join Ramshaw back at the dart board.

The false bravado lasts all of ten seconds, because the man infiltrating my mind on a constant rotation is standing in the hall, leaning up against the wall, looking more perfect than I ever remember him being. Is it the soft lighting? The mysterious shadows hiding part of his handsome face? A combination of the two?

Who the hell knows, but my skin tingles and my heart beats faster with just the sight of him.

He watches me the same way I watch him, long seconds ticking between us with neither speaking a word.

Having him across the room in the bar was one thing, something I could eventually distance myself from. Him in front of me, expectant eyes waiting for something? I swallow thickly, a swarm of emotion hitting me right in the chest and look away.

"Goodnight," I whisper before turning to walk away.

"Sophia." His hand brushes my arm, and that single touch has the ability to stop me in my tracks.

My mouth is dry, and I've lost the ability to speak without my words revealing the pain I've been feeling for weeks. I close my eyes, just breathing in his proximity, hating the pain it causes me.

Is this what obsession feels like? It must be, and I hate it, hate every single thing about it.

"Look at me," he pleads.

"I can't." It's true. Even him being this close to me is painful, and the bad thing about it is, I've done this to myself. I've let my mind fixate on this man, knowing from day one that there could never be anything between us. He has his own set of morals guiding him, and if he doesn't want to be with a younger woman, then who the hell am I to try to tempt and tease him into something? Maybe I did violate him that day in the office. Maybe I misread his cues. Maybe he wasn't looking at me in his kitchen that day with desire. Maybe it was disappointment or disgust and I just read it wrong.

"Sophia."

With his hand on my hip, he turns me to face him, but my gaze lingers on his shoes. Why can't he just let me walk by? He doesn't have to tell me again he doesn't want me. He's made it very clear time and time again. Doing it again when I didn't seek out validation is just cruel.

I hold on to that emotion, because every other one I'm feeling would end with tears on my face. My cheek twitches when I look up at him, but he's too close, his deep blue eyes too searching for me to hide a single thing from him. Reading people is his job, and I feel like he can see right through me.

"I miss you." The scent of whiskey on his breath isn't completely off-putting, but it's knowing he wouldn't be standing in this hallway with me had he not been drinking that makes me want to dart away.

"Please," I whisper, and I don't know exactly what I need.

Please feel the same way when you wake up sober?

Please release me from this hold you have on me?

Please make me yours?

"My sheets no longer smell like you." His nose sweeping down the side of my neck is like a lightning bolt to my spine, but he ignores my whimper. "God, how I want to feel you under me, whispering my name."

Other than his hot hand on my hip and his face buried in my hair, he doesn't touch me. He doesn't push his hips against me to prove his attraction, and it feels like another form of manipulation.

My body doesn't care. My heart is pounding, thighs itching for me to rub them together, mind telling me to step further into his space, but his grip tightens on my waist, preventing me from moving.

"I'm so hard for you. I want to spend hours stroking inside of you. I want your teeth marks in my shoulder from pushing into you just a little too deep." I rake my tongue between my teeth just to feel the pressure. "I'm always hard for you. Every day at the station. Every time I see you or you walk by."

"Colton." My fingers tangle in the front of his shirt, and I can't decide if the best course of action is to push him away or pull him closer.

"I hate the weekends when I don't get to see you. I hate knowing that after next week, I may never get to see you again."

His words are a crushing blow. I've been both looking forward to and dreading the end of my internship.

"I need you."

"Stop." I decide pushing him away is best. "No more fucking games."

He blinks down at me, but I refuse to guess what he's thinking. I'm not willing to take the chance of him getting what he wants while horny and drunk only to backpedal with regret tomorrow.

"Soph." He steps in closer, but I spin away from him.

"No more, Colton."

My back is no longer straight, my head no longer held high when I walk out of the back hallway. Defeated, I skirt past Ramshaw and head straight for the tables where I know I'll be safe. Colton may want me in the moment, but there isn't a man in this bar that's willing to go through half a dozen scary bikers to get laid.

Jinx nods at me when I pass to sit in the empty seat against the wall before continuing his conversation with Rocker, both of them here because Simone is tending bar tonight. I take an offered beer, but spend the next half hour peeling the label rather than drinking it. I want to leave, but the three beers in my system keep my ass planted on the bar stool. It doesn't appear anyone is ready to head out, and that means I'm stuck until they are. Just because my night is ruined doesn't mean I'm going to do the same for someone else.

"Everything okay?"

"Yes," I answer Cannon. "Having a good night?"

"Always a good night," he answers, drawing Rivet closer to his side.

I tried kissing this man when they were in the middle of figuring what they meant to each other. Of course I didn't know that was going on because they were keeping their private lives private, but not once has she looked at me with jealousy. It's something I've always been grateful for. Drama at the clubhouse isn't an anomaly, but I've never wanted to be in the middle of it. As I watch her look up at Cannon like he's the best thing on the planet, I realize she isn't jealous because I was never competition for her. I don't know if it's because she's so sure about herself or if she knows I'm just not good enough to be loved by anyone.

And of course I blame Colton for the self-depreciating attitude because I never felt this way before him.

I swipe the now label-less bottle from the table in front of me and turn the thing up.

Chapter 17

Colton

"What are you doing?"

"What do you mean?" Mom asks, once again looking around me to the driveway.

Rick chuckles and walks past us into the house.

"Just you two today?"

I frown. "Like always. Expecting someone else?"

She shrugs, turning her disappointed face around and following my son into the house. "More like hoping."

"Did he bring her?" Dad calls from the kitchen.

Instead of going in there to face an inquisition, I take my ass to the living room and turn on the television.

"They're talking about Sophia," Rick helpfully offers as he plops down beside me with a soda in his hand.

"I know who they're talking about," I mutter.

They pulled this shit the Sunday after they met her at my house, as well as every family meal after. I knew it was coming, and for the first time since high school, I thought about not showing up today.

"Just you two?" Dad asks, walking into the living room, wiping his hands on a dish towel.

"Don't sound so disappointed." I don't pull my eyes from the television. The car insurance commercial is more interesting than a repeat of this conversation.

"Lunch is in five minutes. We expected you sooner," Dad goads, but he isn't going to get a rise out of me.

I may not have stayed home to avoid this, but I've been coming later and later each week in an attempt to lessen the time spent with them, wondering why I once again showed up alone.

"Better go wash up," Rick says, slapping my thigh and deserting me with my old man.

Ten minutes later, because Dad's time management skills aren't the best, we're settling around the dining room table with a full spread in front of us.

"Nice," Rick says, rubbing his hands together like he's never seen food before in his life and he's overwhelmed with the selection.

"Are you feeding him regularly?" Mom asks as my son reaches for a bowl of mashed potatoes.

"Every meal is like this." Rick piles the potatoes high before reaching for the platter of baked chicken. "He probably has worms or something."

My son is no longer affected by our joking. Like clockwork, this also happens every week. We all smile, watching him load his plate up. At thirty-five, I know he'll be my only child and as the only grandchild, neither my parents nor myself take this young man for granted.

"Did Sophia have other plans today?" Mom asks with a smile as she passes the potatoes to me.

"I don't know what Sophia's plans were today, Mother."

She scoffs at the formal designation, but she either doesn't take the hint that I don't want to have this conversation yet again or she doesn't care.

"We liked her," Dad offers.

"I know."

"She seems very smart."

I take a deep breath. "She is."

"Very mature—"

"She's twenty-one."

"—for her age," Mom continues. "Twenty-one?"

My eyes lift to hers. "Yes. She's still in college."

"I thought she was in a graduate program."

"Nope, undergrad." Maybe this will be enough to put an end to these conversations.

"Her age really isn't an issue," Dad adds.

"But she's probably not ready for something serious," Mom interjects.

"I'm not ready for something serious," I mutter around a mouthful of potatoes.

"She's definitely not ready to be a mom to a teenage son."

Rick chuckles before muttering, "MILF," under his breath.

I kick him under the table, giving him a glare that he knows translates to a conversation we'll be having later. His head drops, eyes back to focusing on scooping food into his mouth.

"She's too young for all of that," I tell my parents.

"Some would argue that nineteen was too young to become a father, but you did an amazing job with Rick."

My mom smiles at me before looking at my son.

"I am kind of perfect, Dad."

I narrow my eyes at him. My parents affection for the kid is in no short supply.

"Keep it up and you'll be on the roof cleaning gutters when we get home," I threaten, aiming my fork in his direction to get my point across.

"So it's just sex then?"

I sputter around a bite of green beans and glare at my mom.

Rick wheezes, clearly choking on his own food, but at this point in the conversation, it's every man for himself. Dad claps Rick on the back, but his eyes stay on me, expectant and waiting for an answer.

Geez, it's like sophomore year all over again. That time I snuck a girl in my bedroom for a make-out session—didn't even make it to third base, if anyone is wondering—and I spent four hours at this very table having the dreaded birds-and-bees talk a year too late.

"I haven't had sex with her," I inform them, uncaring that my son is sitting at the table with me.

As a young father, I've never kept anything hidden from him, and now is no different. I don't flaunt sexual relationships in front of him, but I also don't hide the fact that I've had relations since he was born. Not even my parents preach the no sex before marriage, so a conversation about sex isn't exactly taboo in this household.

"She was half-naked in your clothes."

I glare at Dad, begging him to get Mom to stop talking, but there's a smile that says *no way, I'm just as curious for the answer* playing on his lips.

"She wasn't half-naked," I argue. "She had boxers on under the shirt."

"Your boxers?" Mom continues. "I'm not a prude. I don't care that—"

"I didn't sleep with her," I snap, taking a deep breath to calm down. Not because I'm honestly upset with them, but because of the regret I've been plagued with for the last several weeks. My behavior at the bar the night before last was atrocious, and the anxiety I feel having to go to work tomorrow and once again apologize has left me with minimal tolerance today. "She had been drinking. She called for a ride and didn't want to go home. I let her stay at my place."

"In your bed," Dad clarifies, and it's official, I'll be skipping family brunch next week.

"If you recall the blanket and pillow on the recliner, you can deduce yourselves that I slept there, not in the bed with her."

"You two looked cozy in the kitchen when we walked in."

I clench the edge of the table, knowing that getting up and storming out would not be a very good example for my son.

"Dad struck out," the little traitor says. "I bet I have a better chance with her."

Mom gasps and Dad chuckles when I lift the bread roll from the edge of my plate and throw it at his head. He ducks, and it misses him, of course, but the message is clear. He smiles around a bite of potatoes, and I can't help the twitch of humor in my own mouth.

The kid is right. I struck out. Big time. What I thought was best doesn't seem to be working out the way I had hoped. Wanting her has never been the issue. My desire for Sophia Anderson has only grown since the first time she walked into my office looking like a naughty professor. It's knowing her life would become something she never pictured if we were to make that leap.

Mom is also right, she isn't ready to be a mother to a teenage son, and that's exactly what would happen if things grew serious between us. I'd never ask that of her. Most importantly, I'd never bring a woman into my son's life only to have her leave when she got bored. We've already been hurt like that once, and I won't let it happen again.

"We work together," I say after a long silence. "That's it. We haven't gotten together, and we aren't going to be getting together."

"That's a shame," Mom whispers, but I think she can see that the conversation is getting to me.

"Can we talk about something else?"

"Of course," Dad agrees. "Rick, let's talk about those videos I saw on Tik Tak."

Rick groans, and it's my turn to laugh.

"It's *Tik Tok*, Gramps. We've been over this."

The spotlight stays on my son for the rest of the day, and when we finally leave because we're doing the gutters today, I have a smile on my face. There's still a chance I'll skip next week's family meal, but at least I got a little reprieve today.

"The gutters? Really, Dad?" Rick whines an hour later when I tell him to get the ladder out of the garage.

"I'll get the highest parts," I say, not flinching when he complains again. "But you'll be in big trouble if I ever hear you say another derogatory word about any woman again. Shit like you said at dinner should never leave your mouth, not in front of me, your grandparents, or your friends. I raised you to have more respect than that."

"She's hot as fuck, Dad. People should know."

"People know, Rick." I grind my teeth together. "Everyone who looks at her knows, but being disrespectful isn't going to cut it. Keep that shit to yourself."

"Yes, sir," he mutters before walking toward the garage.

My words from the other night slam into me like a tsunami.

I'm so hard for you. I want to spend hours stroking inside of you. I want your teeth marks in my shoulder from pushing into you just a little too deep. I'm always hard for you. Every day at the station. Every time I see you or you walk by.

God, I hope he turns into a better man than me.

Chapter 18

Sophia

"That's all I have for now. Be safe."

Patrol officers scatter after Monahan ends the beginning-of-shift briefing. Several hover near the coffee pot, waiting to fill up their travel mugs before hitting the streets, and I hang back in the corner of the room like I have been doing every morning for the last couple of weeks.

Ramshaw winks at me before leaving the room. Thankfully, he doesn't ask me why I disappeared Friday evening. I was drunk before Cannon finally gave me a ride back to my house, and both Saturday and Sunday were spent with a hangover. Not my finest moment. Even Dad kept his distance, which was a blessing.

Since helping Colton clear his caseload, I've been asked to help a couple of the other detectives at the station, and I'm happy for the distraction. I'm not going out on calls, but paperwork is a never-ending thing for police. At least helping them type notes and submit reports keeps them on the streets and helping those that need them.

Colton was late once again this morning, sneaking into the briefing mere minutes before it was over. I try to keep my eyes on the folder in front of me, but my other senses track him across the room, picking up bits and pieces of conversation he's having with Gaffey.

All too soon, he leaves the breakroom, and I'm left feeling equal parts relieved and saddened. We need to have a conversation about what happened Friday night, but I just don't have the stomach for it today, or any day in the near future for that matter.

My work, the laundry list of things to get done handed to me by Chief Monahan this morning, ends too quickly. I don't know if he's only giving bits and pieces of the work to me to keep me from getting overwhelmed or he just doesn't realize how efficient I've become with my tasks since starting my internship.

It's not even noon and I'm done. To buy more time in my effort to avoid Colton, I head to the mailroom. I catch the woman who works in here leaving with a quick smile, and I want to hang my head in defeat. My intention to keep busy has been thwarted by her own efficiency. I grab Gaffey's mail, as well as Colton's and head out. Haden isn't in his office when I drop his off, so I head back to the breakroom to sort through Colton's. Strangely, detectives, as well as some patrol officers, get all sorts of weird mail, and I've wondered more than once if some people working here aren't using the police station as their permanent address. I toss several clothing magazines in the trash before opening a simply addressed letter, frowning at the sloppy handwriting before even reading the words. Inmates from the jail are known to spend their time writing letters to arresting officers, the chief, and often times, probation officers, something I learned early on after a conversation with people at a crime scene.

My head tilts, eyes scanning the letter, but then it hits me exactly what it is that I'm holding in my hand. Threats aren't new, but I've never seen a letter written with such graphic terms. The letter goes into the heinous ways he's going to torture Colton if his demands aren't met. I don't know what the person wants because I don't get that far without having to look away.

On trembling legs, I leave the rest of Colton's mail on the table and head straight to his office. I don't bother knocking on his door, and it takes more than one try to get the doorknob to work in my shaking hand.

"Sophia?" Colton looks up from his computer screen, concern drawing his brows together. "What's wrong?"

Unable to answer him, I shove the paper in his direction. At first, he doesn't take it, keeping his eyes on me and trying to assess the situation.

"L-look," I beg. "It's bad."

"Lay it on the desk," he advises, but he doesn't reach for it. "Was there anything else in the envelope? Did it feel gritty or damp?"

"No," I tell him. "Just the one piece of paper."

I pull my hand back once the letter lands on his desk.

"Don't do that," he instructs, reaching for me when I try to lift my trembling hand to my face. "You'll need to wash your hands."

"It's f-fine. There was nothing on the paper."

"Can't be too sure."

Only now do I realize he's holding my hand, and I hate the way the warmth of his touch has a calming effect. It only makes me want to be closer to him, to take more from him than he's willing to offer.

"You're shaking." His grip on my hand tightens.

Looking up at him, I have the urge to touch his face, but I know I can't. Not only is there a concern for what might be on my hands, but he doesn't want that from me.

"Come here."

I don't resist when he pulls me to his chest. Instinctively, my arms go around his back, tangling in the fabric of his shirt as he holds me close.

"It's nothing," he assures me. "We get these all the time."

"He said he's going to kill you, your family, and your dog."

"I don't have a dog, Sophia."

"But you have a family." The memories of the scenes we've worked and the devastation those people had in their eyes with the loss of a child, I can't imagine that same fate for him.

"He doesn't have a clue about my family, baby."

I cling to him tighter.

"Shh, I've got you."

It sounds like a promise, and God, how I wish it were true. I tremble even more, my knees threatening to give out. I feel like such a child right now. I've gone to and assisted on several deaths in the last six weeks, but at the moment, I feel the most vulnerable. Maybe it's because it's my own life in turmoil right now and I don't have the ability to close my eyes and distance myself from it, or maybe it's simply his proximity and finally being in his arms.

I open my mouth to beg him to feel the same way right now while he's sober that he felt Friday night, but a sob comes out instead.

"Baby," he whispers, his face buried in my hair. "Everything is fine."

He couldn't be more wrong.

Fine is subjective. Yeah, nothing may come from the letter. His family may not be in real danger, but I'm not fine. I haven't been *fine* for a very long time.

"I miss you, too," I confess, the admission coming easier since he isn't looking into my tear-soaked eyes.

He holds me tighter, the embrace transitioning from comforting to something a little more carnal.

"All of those things you mentioned at *Jake's*, I want those, too."

More than I could even admit out loud.

Fingers tangle in my hair, his hips moving closer until his entire body is pressed against mine. The stiff length of him presses against my lower belly, and it takes all of my strength not to moan his name.

The threatening letter forgotten, I move my hips only slightly.

"Sophia." The grip in my hair tightens as he tugs, my face coming away from his chest to look up into his eyes.

His teeth dig into his lower lip as he assesses my face. I know my makeup is smeared, cheeks stained with tears, but he's looking at me like I'm the most beautiful woman in the world. It's the same way he looked when I first walked out of the restroom at *Jake's*.

"Are you sure?" he whispers, and all I can do is nod. "If you're not—"

"Matthews, I need—"

We both freeze, and even though my back is to the door, I know that Chief Monahan just caught us in an embrace.

"In my office, Matthews. Now."

I watch silently as Colton pulls on a pair of gloves, picks the letter up off his desk on the corner, and leaves. He doesn't look back or say a word to assure me that everything is going to be fine. If anything, he looks relieved to be walking away.

I wipe angry fingers at the renewed tears on my face, uncaring of what could be on my hands. It can't hurt me any more than I'm hurting right now.

Once my face is dried, I head straight back to my little corner of the breakroom, although I don't know how long I'll be here. I may very well be minutes away from getting shown the damn door. Monahan walked in on a private moment, one that had no business happening at the police station. He's the boss. The one that approved my internship, and he's also the man that can easily yank it right out from under me a week and a half before graduation.

Chapter 19

Colton

My heart is pounding more than it did when I had to sit my parents down to tell them that I got a girl pregnant after a drunken bad decision, but I'll face this the exact same way. I haven't backed down or made excuses for a bad decision in my life.

She's not a bad decision.

And yet, I somehow managed to take advantage of her while she was upset.

"Fuck," I mumble as I step into Monahan's office.

"Close the door." He doesn't move from his leaning position against the front of his desk. "Have a seat."

With my gloved hands, I place the letter that upset Sophia on the corner of a side table and do as he asks. I respect the hell out of this man, and since I know I deserve a dressing down, I'm gonna sit here and fucking take it. Hopefully, it doesn't end in the request for my gun and badge.

"We have a no fraternization policy."

"We do." Not that anyone follows it. Two of the women in dispatch are dating the same damn patrol officer, and it makes for some really intense investigations some days.

"Sophia Anderson was required to complete the same paperwork with human resources as if she were being hired for a permanent position with the department."

"Okay." I didn't know that, but it makes total sense. We deal with some pretty serious stuff up here.

"You can't start something with her while she's working here."

I don't miss the fact that he doesn't say never.

"Her father wouldn't be very happy to know you were taking advantage of his daughter while she was trying to finish her school year."

"I'm not taking advantage of her, Chief."

Yet, only moments ago I was berating myself for feeling like I did.

"So it's a mutual thing?"

"There's no *thing*, Chief."

"I've been a cop for as long as you've been alive, son. I know what I saw. She's out of here in less than two weeks. You're going to need to hit the brakes on it until she's out of here."

"Chief." He holds his hand up to silence me, and my jaw snaps shut.

"I have to admit, I'm a little disappointed because I want that girl working here. She's the best intern we've ever had. I can't employ her, knowing you're having a relationship with her." His eyes narrow. "Just how far have you taken things with her."

I glare back at him, my agitation at not being able to explain getting the best of me. "Are you asking as my boss or as her father's friend?"

He pauses, clearly deciding which direction he wants to go. "Both."

I huff a laugh. No middle ground, I see.

"I'm supervising her while she does her internship, as I was told to do."

"And your supervision requires daily hugs?" He scoffs. "You're not fooling me, Matthews. I'm old and married, but I still know a gorgeous woman when I see one."

"I'm not—"

"And lying is only going to piss me off more."

I twist my jaw, taking slow breaths through my nose and releasing them out of my mouth. "May I speak?"

His arms cross in front of his chest, and it's a clear sign he isn't going to be very receptive of anything I say. It almost makes me wish I was guilty of what he's accusing me of. At least it would make everything worth it.

"Sophia goes through my mail. It's one of the things she offered to do so I could focus more of my time and energy clearing cases. Which, I might add, has happened at an astonishing rate the last six weeks." I point to the letter I dropped on the side table, but his assessing eyes stay on me. "She freaked out when she opened one envelope and found that letter. I haven't read the entire thing, but I scanned it on the walk from my office. It's graphic, extremely detailed about how I'm going to die and how my entire family, including my dog, is going to be tortured."

"You don't have a dog," Monahan says, and it brings a smile to my face. I have more in common with this man than I want to admit.

"I know. Sophia didn't know that." It's my first lie since I walked in here. "She was terrified, shaking, and crying."

Okay, so she wasn't crying until I pulled her to my chest, but he'll never know the true sequence of events.

"I've been thinking for weeks that she wasn't ready to just be thrown into the type of cases I work. Most patrol officers don't see the kind of stuff she's been dealing with while working with me. It's too much for her. I don't know what tipped the scale today, but she was nearly inconsolable. I hugged her. It was a comforting move, and I think her father would be okay with that."

Another lie. Dominic Anderson would never be okay with me having my hands on his daughter for any reason.

"I wondered the same thing before I put her with you." Monahan finally drops his arms, the guarded stance slowly fading away. He circles his desk before falling into his office chair. "I made the assumption that she was just as strong as the man who raised her, but it's clear I fucked up."

"I don't think it was the letter on its own, but it just came at the right time."

"We need to distance her from the cases."

"What?" I snap my eyes back to him. "No."

I've had enough distance from her, all of it emotional. I won't survive actual physical distance.

"Your objection makes my mind go right back to my original way of thinking."

Jesus, fuck. I can't win.

"She has seven days after today. I think if you pull her from my cases now, she's going to think she's done something wrong."

"She hasn't," he agrees. "But I don't want the girl losing sleep over the shit she's seeing in the field."

He was probably more focused on my arms around her when he came in my office, but I know if she turned around to face him, he would've seen the darkness under her eyes. Like he said, he's been doing this job for a long time. I don't know if those smudges are there because of me or the job. Would it make me a complete asshole if it made me feel slightly better if she was losing sleep over me the way I have been with her?

Probably.

"Seven more days, Chief. She's planning to go to grad school. I think she made up her mind on her own that she isn't ready for this line of work."

His hand rubs at the stubble forming on his chin as he thinks about it.

"She can help work scenes with you if you get called out, but I don't want her spending much time with the victims. You're right about most cops having the shit she's seen spread out over years and years. I think she's just been too close to a bunch of bad shit at too high of a rate." He points toward the letter I brought in here. "Ease her fears by arresting the fucker who mailed that fucking letter first."

"You got it, Chief."

I stand from the chair and turn around to grab the letter.

"And, Matthews?" I turn to face him again. "I don't doubt anything you told me in here today, but I'm not a damn fool either. There was more than comfort in your eyes earlier. Seven more days until she's out of here. Keep your fucking hands off of her at least that damn long, would you?"

"Yes, sir."

"And even after," he continues when I have my back to him, "you better be a hundred percent sure that whatever is going on between the two of you is worth sacrificing the connection this community has with the Cerberus MC. Fucking around with one of the princesses could sever ties we've spent decades building."

Well, fuck.

Sophia isn't in my office when I return, and it only takes me five minutes and a quick conversation with Gaffey to discover she went home because she wasn't feeling well. It's probably for the best.

Her words mix with the chief's warning in my head as I read the sent letter over and over and over. The dick that wrote the letter wants his brother released from jail. Of course Dennis Milton, the man who shot his girlfriend three times in the chest has a crazy brother that thinks threats will get him released. Just another fucking day in the office as far as I'm concerned. Since the idiot all but signed his own name to the damn thing, it doesn't take long to get a warrant from a judge to have him arrested. I hand the task off to a patrol unit because I know I'll strangle the fucker for scaring Sophia. That little pesky fact and that technically I'm considered a victim in the case, which makes me being the arresting officer a conflict of interest.

Unbidden and like always, my thoughts drift back to thoughts of her. From the warning Monahan gave me, I know he thinks whatever I would start with Sophia wouldn't be worth it in the long run, but as much as I want to know what she sounds like in bed, as much as I want to know the exact shade of her nipples and the way the inside of her thighs taste like, I also want to know a million other non-sexual things.

I want to know how she likes her steak cooked and if she prefers warm showers over hot showers. Does she like ranch salad dressing or does she have more exotic tastes like a poppy seed vinaigrette? Would she smile or be a sore loser if Rick beat her at *Monopoly*? Does she prefer the beach over the mountains? Would she stick around when things got tough?

I swallow, emotion rising up my throat, at the memory of dream-Sophia smiling up at me with our newborn daughter in her arms.

Would it be worth it?

If she were in a position in her life to share those things with me, then I know without a shadow of a doubt that Sophia Anderson would be worth every single second of my life.

Chapter 20

Sophia

"We're waiting for the arson investigator," the fireman says, his eyes still on the smoldering building in front of us. "I can't give the official word, but I've been on the job for thirty years and I can tell you there's no way this isn't an arson case."

"We have three deceased on the second floor," the voice on the radio on his turnout jacket says. "We're still working on clearing the third."

"I need you to stay back," Colton says as he walks toward the building. "It's dangerous."

"If it's dangerous for me," I say, snagging his shoulder before he can get away from me, "then it's dangerous for you, too."

"It's too dangerous for both of you. No one goes in until we're sure of the structural stability," the fireman says, his eyebrow going up when something inside of the structure collapses. "See?"

An echo of voices come over the radio, letting the fireman know they're all safe and giving technical details for what's happening inside.

"Wait in the car with me?" Colton offers when I cross my arms over my chest, making it clear I'm not going anywhere if he's planning to work this scene.

We both concede, the heat from the sun as well as the fire becoming a little too much for comfort.

It's the middle of May, and I'm three days, including today, away from ending my internship with the Farmington Police Department. Technically, I'm done. My final grades, including the one for my internship posted last night. The writeups from both Colton and Chief Monahan complimentary enough to earn me an A.

And honestly, it was difficult to show up to the station today because the last week has been much like the weeks prior. Despite the connection I know we shared in his office, Colton has kept his distance. I haven't pursued anything either because it was clear with the way he avoided me the next day that he no longer felt what I presumed he was feeling.

Since I already have a pit in my stomach as my last days draws closer, I knew I couldn't stay away and spend these last couple of days with him. He's attending my graduation party at the clubhouse on Saturday, and I've cried myself to sleep several times knowing that may be the last time I'll see him.

The air conditioner runs in the car, but it doesn't stop sweat from beading between my shoulder blades. It has more to do with the words I want to say to him rather than heat that's causing the reaction, but I just don't know where to start. I know I need to lay it all out before my last day, but sitting in a car while waiting for the death investigation of at least three people makes it seem disrespectful.

Instead of talking, I watch the firefighters work the scene, still having to put out small fires popping up in hotspots.

"I always thought firefighters and cops hated each other."

Colton chuckles. "It's more of a brotherly competition than true hatred, like a school rivalry."

And there he goes breaking down information in a juvenile way to remind me of our age difference once again.

"Detectives get more animosity from patrol officers than we ever get from the fire department."

"Hmm."

I can feel his eyes on the side of my face, but I can't look in his direction. Terror keeps me from opening my mouth. Everything he says is true. There's a nearly thirteen-year difference between our ages. To most that would make him too old. He has a nearly grown son for heaven's sake. I still live at home with my parents, and I'm more than likely not even done with college. If I pursue my master's degree, I'll still be in college by the time Rick goes into college. Having a son and a girlfriend in college at the same time? What man wants that? What could he possibly see in me other than sexual release? What in the world do I have to offer a man like him?

Nothing.

That's the simple answer, but I can still sense his eyes on me, as if he's waiting expectantly for me to say something to him.

"When I showed up to your office that first day, I really thought things were going to be different." I roll my head on the back of the seat and finally look at him.

His eyes dart to my mouth, but that's not a new thing. I never doubted his sexual attraction to me, he's just more able to keep his desires in check than the college boys I've been with were.

"I did, too." His words are soft as I blink up at him. "I was certain you were going to get in the way or flake on me by Friday. You've legitimately become an amazing addition to our department the last two months."

Not even close to what I was thinking would happen that first week. A noise outside of the car draws his attention, and we both watch as the firefighters continue their work.

"I was certain I'd fuck you by the end of the week."

My heart stops with my vocal confession. Colton's hands grip the steering wheel tighter, his knuckles turning white from the pressure.

"That so?" he asks after a long silence, but he doesn't look at me.

"You were disappointed when you found out who I was."

"I was," he agrees, and it hurts a little more than I thought it would. "I was also hard as fuck the second you darkened my door. I spent the first five minutes of our conversation wondering if I actually had it in me to fuck someone in my office."

"You wonder that often?"

He turns his head, fiery eyes meeting mine, and I feel his embrace even though he isn't touching me.

"Not once until the day you showed up."

I swallow. "And since then?"

"Every fucking day."

He doesn't break eye contact, and his gaze doesn't drift from mine.

"Why are we avoiding each other if it's what we both want?"

"Is it what you want?" His eyes dart between mine. "You want to be a quick fuck on my desk?"

"No." My eyes burn with the implication. "I want it long and hard. Deep. Fast."

"Jesus Christ, Sophia." He pulls his eyes away, adjusting himself in his slacks.

"We've been dancing around each other for the last two months. In your kitchen. At *Jake's*."

"You think I don't fucking know that?" He sounds angry, but I don't get the feeling that he's mad at me. He's not blaming me for the attraction, and if I had to guess, I'd bet he blames himself fully. According to him, he's the adult after all. He's the one who should be able to control himself, no matter the slipups he's had recently. And that's exactly what *Jake's* was, a mistake, something he can blame on alcohol and correct by not drinking when I'm near.

"Are we really just going to walk away from each other at the end of the week and pretend we haven't been getting ourselves off with the thoughts of each other?"

His eyes squeeze shut, and it's the best confession he can give me. At least I'm not the only one. At least he shares some mutual obsession about me.

"I respect your father too much to cross that line with you."

"You don't even know my father."

"The department respects him too much," he amends.

"I'm a grown woman."

"I'm very well aware."

"I get to make decisions about my life without having to consult my parents."

"I'm a parent," he says as if I need reminding, his head swiveling back toward me. Gone is the needy look in his eyes, having been replaced with desolation and loss. "I have to think about Rick."

"I would never cross a line with him. I told you—"

"The thought didn't even cross my mind, Sophia. I want you to know that, but his happiness and stability is my number one concern. I can't bring another woman into our lives only for her to leave."

"You were heartbroken when she left," I whisper.

"I think kids deserve two parents."

"You loved her."

"I—" His hands scrape over the top of his head before falling right back to the steering wheel, and I can't help but wonder if his grip there is so he's not tempted to reach for me. "I should have. A man should love his wife."

"But you didn't?"

"We were young. I wasn't in a relationship with her when we hooked up. When she came to me three months later to tell me she was pregnant, if felt like the right thing to do even though neither one of us really wanted it."

"Your parents were okay with you marrying so young?" I know my dad would be very vocal if the situation happened in our family.

"No, but we were both eighteen. They didn't really have a say. I wanted to give Rick what I had growing up, two parents in a happy home. She was gone before I knew that love, not marriage, was the foundation for that. Failure was inevitable."

"I'm not her."

"You don't know that."

I want to grab a handful of his hair and shake it until he sees reasoning. "I would never walk away from a child, Colton."

He nods as if he understands, but it doesn't seem to change his mind. It's not only age keeping us apart. His mind is so warped from Rick's mother leaving and deserting them both that I don't think there's a thing I can say to convince him otherwise.

His relationship with her was over before it began, and it seems it's the same for us.

"I would never hurt you like that," I vow.

His eyes meet mine, and all the walls he's put up over the last couple of months fade away. He's no longer hiding a single piece of himself, and the sight makes my chin quiver with unleashed emotion.

"I'd never give you the chance."

And the shutters go back into place.

"Okay." I nod in understanding. "I won't beg you, no matter how much my body wants you, how much I throb for you, or how much time I've spent at night thinking about you and what your touch on my skin would feel like. I won't waste another second of your time trying to convince you that I'm worth the risk."

Before I start to cry, I open the car door and get out.

I approach the fireman we were speaking with earlier.

"I have a few questions about burn patterns in arson cases." I pull my little notebook and pen out of my pocket. "I was hoping you could share a little of your expertise."

"Sure thing," he says before going into a long description of accelerants.

I may only have a few days left in my internship, but I plan to learn everything I can until I'm done.

Since I already know what a broken heart feels like, I might as well add arson investigation on top of the pile.

The rest of the shift is uneventful, and even though I didn't get very close, I know it's going to take several washes for the scent of smoke to leave my clothes.

My phone rings on the way home, and despite what I'm feeling where Colton is involved, I smile when I see Izzy's name on my dash.

"Hey!" I say when the call connects, hoping she can't hear the waver in my voice.

"Are you sitting down?"

"I mean, technically. I'm driving. What's up?"

"Park somewhere."

"I'm almost home."

"Do not go home yet."

I pull my foot from the gas and slow down. "You're scaring me."

"I'm scared myself. Tell me when you park."

Silence fills my car as I drive, a million horrible scenarios coming at me in flashes.

"Parked," I say as I pull into a gas station and park around the back so I'm out of the way of traffic. "Fucking talk, Izzy."

She sighs instead.

"Is everything okay?"

"Not really." A sob escapes her throat. "I'm pregnant."

And that wasn't even at the top of the list of things I conjured.

"Wh-what?"

"My dad is going to kill me."

"He won't." Hound doesn't have a leg to stand on. He got Gigi pregnant at nineteen.

"I didn't even know you lost your virginity."

"It was—" Another sob. "That same night."

"You got pregnant by the guy you lost your virginity to? Fuck, bad sex and a baby. Talk about a double whammy."

"It wasn't bad sex!" she screams, and my eyes widen at her hysterical response.

"Okay, sorry," I mutter. "What did the baby daddy say?"

Silence.

"Izzy?"

Silence.

"Isabella Roze Montoya, you better tell me everything."

And she does. She tells me about meeting this guy, how they hit it off, how charming he was, how they spent some time together. It sounds like a fairy tale—a girl meeting the man of her dreams—but then she admits, she never got his first name, oddly only his last, and even if she did, she doesn't want him to know about the baby. She knows more, and for some reason she doesn't feel comfortable talking about it right now. I'll get the truth out of her eventually because there are red flags all over this situation, but she's distraught and not willing to open up fully.

"What are you going to do?"

"I don't know," she whispers. "I just don't know."

Chapter 21

Colton

The easy smile on her pretty face forces one on mine. I'm standing off to the side of her little going away party at the office, and due to the in-and-out nature of law enforcement, it's been going on for nearly two hours, patrol officers and other detectives stopping in when they get a break from duty.

I'm not the only one she's charmed with her quick wit, intelligence, and work ethic. Everyone, from patrol and dispatch to Ethel, the woman who works part time in the mailroom, has a quick smile and some small token or gift for her last day. The cake Monahan's wife made, as well as the small spread of finger foods has been destroyed.

Both Ramshaw and that douche Dresden offer to carry her with them on a patrol shift. She turns Dresden down cold, giving him a look scathing enough that I don't think the man will ever approach her again. Ramshaw doesn't get the same treatment, and he walks away with a wide grin on his face, winking at me in victory as he leaves to do final paperwork before he gets off shift. I wonder if it was the jogging leggings with the hidden gun holster he bought for her that tipped the scale in his favor.

The small box in my back pocket burns my skin, but I don't want to give her the gift in front of everyone else. She's less than an hour away from being free and clear of the police department, and I'm hoping to get just a few minutes of her time alone before she walks out of here for good.

Unable to watch everyone fawn over her without approaching her myself, I edge out of the room. Her purse is still in my office, so I know she'll have to come in here eventually. The wait—forty-five minutes to be exact—is spent with me staring at the blank screen of my computer. Cases are cleared, and with any luck, I can make it through the weekend without getting called out, but that's highly unlikely.

She doesn't look surprised to see me in my office, but she doesn't speak when she reaches for her purse on the shelf either. My throat feels like it's going to close up.

"Sophia," I say, standing and coming around my desk to be near her.

"It was nice working with you, Detective Matthews."

A harsh breath slips past my lips at the formality. I step around her and close the door, turning back around to find her back ramrod stiff, eyes looking over my shoulder. If it weren't for the trembling grip she has on the strap of her purse, I'd think she was indifferent.

"I got this for you." I pull the box from my back pocket, frowning down at the rumpled state of it.

"I didn't expect a gift from you." Her tone suggests that she doesn't even want it.

"Please take it," I beg when she doesn't reach for it.

Courtesy wins out as she places her purse in the chair in front of my desk and clasps the box.

"Thank you." Her bottom lip trembles when she pulls the lid off, revealing the tiny charm hanging from a delicate chain.

"It's—"

"Saint Michael, Patron Saint of Police." She smiles weakly down at the necklace. "It's beautiful. Thank you."

"To keep you safe while you finish school."

"I won't go back until the spring. I missed the deadline for the fall application."

"What are your plans for—" I shake my head. It's none of my business. "Never mind."

She smiles softly. "I should..."

"Yeah."

I don't think I can watch her walk out of here. I know she's going to be in town, even longer now since her college plans have been delayed, but it feels like a forever goodbye. I didn't even have to get this woman in my bed for her to break my heart. I'm such a damn fool.

"Thank you for everything." She offers her hand, but it's too formal, too impersonal, and I pull her against my chest for a hug, my nose immediately diving into her fragrant hair.

I plan to let her go, but five seconds later, I'm still clinging to her. Another five go by, and I know it's time to step back, but I feel her fingers curl into my clothes, making me hold her tighter.

Can I watch her walk away without having gotten a real taste of her mouth? God, I was a fool that day I pushed her away, and I've been a fool every damn day since.

She breaks the contact like I knew she would, her eyes sparkling with tears. Without hesitation, I reach up and wipe them away with my thumbs, my body stepping into her rather than giving her the distance I know we both need.

"Colton?"

"Just one?" I ask, swallowing as I focus on her mouth. "One kiss. A good luck, a congratulations, thanks for helping me out the last two months—an I'm going to miss you kiss. Just one?"

She blinks up at me, her eyes searching. "Just one?"

I nod.

"Can you make it a good one? One I'll remember for the rest of my life?"

God, I could only hope I'll stay in her memory.

I tilt her chin, pausing for the briefest of seconds before my lips meet hers.

The first sweep is soft, a prelude to what we're both wanting. I can't rush this. If one is all we're going to get, I want it to be the best kiss she'll ever have. When asked thirty years from now who made her the most breathless, I want my face in her mind.

My hands leave her face when I press my lips to hers the second time, one gripping her low on her back, drawing her even closer to me, the other tangled in her hair at her nape.

She hums her approval when I nip at her bottom lip, the action making it easy to slip my tongue inside. A million butterflies take flight in my stomach, their wings flapping in a way I've never felt once in my life. It's more than arousal, more than need, more than that tingle in my spine telling me we'd be amazing in bed together.

It's lov—

Damnit! I can't even think of the word in my head because my heart is already halfway to breaking with the loss of her, and she's still in my arms.

I spin the two of us, her tongue sweeping over mine, and press her against my office door. Her amazing tits throb against my chest with each ragged breath she takes, small whimpers escaping her mouth when I push my hips against her. I'm solid, an iron pipe in my slacks, but that isn't what this is about.

I change the angle, delving deeper into her mouth, wanting to crawl inside of her and build a home. When I can no longer resist licking down the column of her neck, I break the kiss and take a step back. Her pink tongue skates over her swollen lips, and the sight is enough to make me groan.

I notice the tremble in my hand when I push a lock of her hair behind her ear.

Without thought, my thumb traces her bottom lip.

"Goodbye," I whisper as I open my office door and then walk away.

Chapter 22

Sophia

I built my college graduation up more than I should have. Instead of it being this huge shining moment, it was hours of sitting and pretending to pay attention while waiting for the entire thing to just be over with.

Tonight is different. Tonight is going to be fun. I have just the right amount of alcohol in my system to smile at everything, and just enough to feel bold at the sight of Colton Matthews standing across the room. He doesn't look uneasy in the clubhouse, but I don't miss the way his eyes roam around the room, taking everything but me in.

I have no doubt he knows where I'm at and would track me across the room if I got up and walked somewhere else. I could go and flirt with the new guys Cerberus hired, but I don't have it in me to waste my time. I told him more than once, I wasn't looking to play games with him. Hell, I was prepared to walk away and count the loss of him as a lesson learned then...

"One kiss. A good luck, a congratulations, thanks for helping me out the last two months—an I'm going to miss you kiss. Just one?"

There's not even half a chance I can stay away from him now because that kiss was *the* kiss. The one that will make everyone after pale in comparison. The one that will haunt my dreams until I get another. There's no walking away after that.

I told him a week and a half ago that I wouldn't beg, but hell that was before knowing what his tongue felt like against mine. Then, I was strong and determined. Now, I'm an addict, and like the letdown after that first taste of heroin, my skin is itching for the next hit.

I pressed a cordial kiss to his cheek when I greeted him upon arrival but begging him to get me out of here at the time didn't happen. There were too many people watching, too many people without an ounce of alcohol in their systems for me to make my move that early in the night.

With confidence, I pull out my phone and shoot off a text.

Me: Still turned on by that kiss.

I turn my phone over in my lap when Izzy shifts beside me.

"Look." I nudge my head in the direction of Delilah and Ivy. They're both fawning over Simone's little boy. "No one around here gets upset about babies."

"Hush," she snaps, looking around the room to make sure no one overheard me.

I watch as Colton pulls his phone from his pocket, but he doesn't send a text back before stuffing it right back in his jeans.

That fucker.

Picking up my phone, I fire off another text. Go big or go home, right?

Me: My pussy is so wet for you.

His head tilts halfway in my direction but he catches himself before looking at me fully. There's a warning there, I just know it, but I'm no longer going to listen to the voice in my head telling me it'll be better if I walk away.

"Who are you texting?" Izzy whispers near my ear.

"Hush," I hiss. "Mind your own business."

"My own business?" She huffs. "Pot. Kettle. Daddy? Really, Soph, aren't you a little old to have Dom's phone number in your phone like that?"

I turn my phone over just as it buzzes in my hand. Then it buzzes again, and again, and again. Izzy is still in my face, so I turn my phone over and hold it comically close to my nose. Before I read the texts, I make a quick scan of the room. Mom and Dad are nuzzling each other like teens during prom. Other than Izzy, no one else is around that I'm worried about.

Daddy: Stop.
Daddy: Please don't do this to me.
Daddy: Fuck.
Daddy: And how am I supposed to explain an erection to your father?

I bite my lips to stave off a smile, my eyes taking in every inch of his massive body. The way he pressed me into his office wall Thursday comes to mind, and I know the man has the strength to pick me up, fuck me hard and not even break a sweat.

"Really?" Izzy squeals. "That's who you're texting?"

"Shhh," I snap.

"Your dad will kill you and him."

Maybe... maybe not.

"You have to try these!" My sister Jasmine sits down on the other side of Izzy, attempting to pass a cheeseburger slider to me, but I'm only hungry for one thing right now.

I ignore her, shooting off another text.

Me: I have a few ideas on how we can solve that problem.

"Oh, God," Izzy groans. In my peripheral vision, I see her hand clutch her stomach. A second later, she's covering her mouth like she's going to be sick and running for the hallway.

"Oh no," Rocker hisses from the sofa only a couple of feet away.

"What's wrong with her?" Hound asks, concerned about his oldest daughter as he walks across the room holding Amelia's tiny hand as she toddles beside him.

"How far along is she?" Simone blurts, and my eyes have to look like saucers.

"Excuse me?" Hound snaps.

My eyes dart around the room—everything but this conversation suddenly more interesting than the glare I know I'm getting from Hound.

"What did you say?" Hound demands again.

"It's the meat. I mean I could be wrong, but the smell of meat makes me sick," Simone explains.

"You're pregnant, too?" I ask, the question slipping out before I can stop it. I slap my hand over my mouth, but the damage is already done.

"She isn't," Hound argues, his head shaking back and forth like saying the words will make them true. "She's too young."

"She's the same age as I was when we got pregnant with Amelia," Gigi says, looking at her husband with a bored expression.

Did Izzy confide in her, too? She doesn't look exactly surprised by the news.

I watch in horror as Hound looks around the room trying to figure out who he's going to kill for touching his daughter. Little does he know the man will never step foot in this clubhouse. Izzy has no interest in tracking down the guy who got her pregnant, and I doubt Hound will ever be able to get the truth out of her.

"No fucking way, man!" Apollo, one of the new Cerberus members says, holding his arms up near his head in mock surrender. "I haven't touched her!"

Ignoring the man's declaration, I watch as Apollo's face turns white when Hound begins to cross the room.

A phone rings, but most people are waiting to see if blood is going to be shed on the clubhouse floor. Like I said, there's always drama around here.

"That's not fucking possible," Lawson hisses, his drink falling to the floor at his feet when he surges up from the couch. "I'll be there."

Lawson is ignoring the mess at his feet and staring down at his phone like it's a bomb ready to explode.

"What's going on?" Delilah asks, her hand clamping on her husband's arm.

"Drew," he whispers, and the entire room goes silent.

Tears instantly burn the backs of my eyes. Drew, Lawson's younger half-brother, is working for the New Mexico State Police. He's only been on the job for a couple of months. Fuck, he's still training to be a cop.

"No. Please, no," I gasp, my lungs refusing to fill completely with air.

Several others around me are having the same reaction.

"No, no," Lawson says, lifting his head and looking around the room. "He hasn't been hurt. Well, not yet, but when I get my hands on him—"

"Then what?" Lawson's dad asks as he steps in closer.

Lawson looks up, despair in his eyes. "He's been arrested by the police."

"Arrested by the police?" Someone scoffs on the other side of the room, and I think it's Cannon, but I can't pull my eyes away from Lawson. "He *is* the police."

"This seems familiar," Griffin mutters, having had his own run-in with law enforcement awhile back. "What's he been picked up for?"

Lawson doesn't pull his eyes from his dad when he answers, "Homicide."

The room erupts in chaos. Even Hound has stopped his pursuit of Apollo.

Questions fly, ones Lawson can't answer, before people start piling out. Kincaid, my Dad, Kid, Snatch, and several other men shuffle a traumatized Lawson and Delilah into the conference room, closing the door with a thunderous bang.

Ivy moves into action, Simone climbing off the couch to help clean up. I'm a robot as I move around the room collecting plates and trash.

"This is your party. You shouldn't be helping." My sister clutches my forearm, pulling the trash bag from my fist. Without even looking, she hangs it out to the side for Tug to take. He presses a kiss to her temple before walking away and picking up where I left off.

When she steps away, my eyes dart around the room. Only I find Colton's back as he heads for the front door instead of spotting him across the room where he was moments ago. Does he really think he can just walk out of here and leave me behind? That is not on the agenda for tonight.

Chapter 23

Colton

I couldn't even imagine getting the news this club just got hit with, and no matter how curious I am, it's not my business. It didn't happen in my jurisdiction because I would've gotten the call about a homicide long before family and friends were notified of a suspect's arrest.

I pull my phone out of my pocket as I leave, just to make sure I didn't miss something while trying to will my dick to deflate after Sophia's damn filthy texts. She's a different level of distraction than I've ever known.

Nope. Nothing. I breathe a sigh of relief. I hope I never have to work a case against a fellow officer, and I'm doubly glad I'm not having to work a case against a man under the protection of the Cerberus MC.

Cool air hits me in the face as I step outside, a sharp relief to the warmth that was filling my cheeks inside the clubhouse. I could blame the abundance of people in the large room, but I know it's the thoughts of that damn temptress in there that's making me warm from head to toe. Hell, even after watching a group of people horrified with bad news, my cock is still semi-interested in what Sophia was offering via text message.

"Detective Matthews!"

I keep walking, knowing if I stop and face her, I'll end up making a huge mistake—one I won't be able to argue against if her dad walks out of the clubhouse.

"Colton!" she snaps when I reach for the door of my truck.

"Go back inside, Sophia."

She shoves me from behind, the surprise of it making me stumble more than the force she's able to manage.

"Turn around." The command makes my cock throb—not because I like being bossed around but from the gall of thinking she can tell me what to do. "I need answers."

"I thought we said just one—"

Jesus, if she tempts me tonight, I won't be able to walk away.

"Not that." My heart deflates. "I need to know what's going on with Drew."

"I don't know anything. It didn't happen here."

"I know, but you're a cop. Use some of that professional courtesy we talked about before and find out."

"From the sounds of it, it's still an open investigation. I can't call the department he's working for and ask for information."

"The State Police," she corrects.

"Especially them," I mutter. "You know how this goes, Sophia. We've worked several cases together from start to finish. If it happened in the last twenty-four hours, there's a good chance the information isn't even in their system. Those men are having to work a case against one of their own, and I can't get involved in that. It could bring heat down on my department."

"Okay." She hangs her head in disappointment, but I know she knows I'm right.

I open the truck door, ready to tell her goodnight although I don't want to, but she shoves past me and climbs across the driver's seat, settling her sexy ass body against the passenger window.

If she leaves here tonight with me, she won't be going home. I know her father already suspects something with the way he glared at me when she pressed her hot, little lips to my cheek in greeting when I arrived. Of course, her mother just smiled at the two of us, but her look was knowing as well. I could be on a damn hitlist already, and I've only been here an hour and a half.

"What are you doing?" I try to hide the smile at her brazen attitude, but it's impossible.

All she does is smile at me.

"How much have you had to drink?"

"Why? Are you wanting to take advantage?"

This little devil.

"Sophia," I warn.

"Yes, Daddy?" She giggles, but her words make my face screw up. "I have you in my phone as Daddy."

I cringe even further. I never considered the woman having daddy issues as reasoning for being attracted to me. "That's disturbing."

"I didn't want my friend to be suspicious," she explains. "Take me home with you, Colton."

Done resisting, done hesitating, I climb in the truck and crank it. A second later, we're leaving Cerberus' property and heading toward my house.

She hums along to the radio, watching out the window rather than engaging me in conversation. Is it possible she's as nervous as I am right now? My heart is racing, sweat dampens my temples, and it's worse than the ten minutes right before I lost my virginity, and I was only nervous then because I didn't know what to expect.

Now, I know how amazing sex can be. I have no doubt sex with Sophia is going to be out of this world, but I'm still freaking out, more from wondering what happens after than from anticipation.

"The light is green," she whispers when I get entranced at the sight of her running her finger back and forth, back and forth over the bottom hem of her dress.

"Right," I say, darting my eyes forward so I don't get us both killed in a traffic accident.

She chuckles, but I only manage a quick look in her direction before focusing back on the road ahead of us.

"What?"

I grin when she laughs again.

"Why are you so nervous?"

"Is it that obvious?"

"You're strumming your fingers on the steering wheel. You have beads of sweat rolling down your neck. Your back is as stiff as a board."

"Very observant, detective."

She laughs even louder at that. "I learned from the best."

"You've been the perfect pupil."

"I bet there are a million more things you can teach me."

Her voice takes on a sultry tone, and my dick takes notice before my brain can even catch up, making me wish I made a checklist of the things I want to do with her tonight.

"Rick isn't home tonight?" she asks when I make the turn into my neighborhood.

"Staying with a friend," I assure her.

In the drive, I put the truck in park, but don't turn off the ignition.

Her legs, tan in the moonlight and a stark contrast to the light color of her dress, hold every ounce of my attention. I haven't seen them bare since that day in my kitchen, and what a damn shame that is. They're perfect, deserving of attention.

"If we go inside—"

"I know," she interrupts, her eyes finding mine in the dim light.

We both knew what was going to happen when I drove away from the clubhouse, but I'm giving her one last chance, one more opportunity to walk away. I can't make her promises. I don't have a crystal ball able to tell me what tomorrow is going to look like for us.

Maybe it's a casual sex thing. Maybe I don't have to worry about Rick getting hurt because she'll only come around when he's gone. Maybe it'll be a one-time thing because we'll find out we aren't even close to being sexually compatible.

I shake my head, answering every one of those questions in an instant. There's nothing casual about what's been stewing between the two of us. Rick will hurt because I'll be hurting if she walks away. There's no way I'll spend only one night inside of this woman.

"What will tomorrow look like?" she asks as if reading my mind. Her fingers tangle in the hem of her dress, but she keeps her eyes locked on mine.

I bite my lip before answering, knowing it could be a moment of truth for us. If she wants something different, I may have to be the one to walk away.

"You mean after I wake you with my cock inside of you?" She swallows, getting distracted with the possibilities.

"Is this a one-time thing?"

"It can't be, Sophia. Nor is it casual. I can't do no-strings attached with you."

"You're sure?"

"A hundred percent. If that's not what you want, I can take you home."

Her eyes flutter as she looks at me. "I'm right where I want to be."

Chapter 24

Sophia

Not casual.

I think I hesitated for so long because this was my top fear.

I'm not afraid of what my family will think or the possible backlash of dating an older man. My mom is younger than my dad. My entire life I've witnessed what love should look like. Does that mean I have daddy positivity rather than daddy issues because of my childhood? Maybe.

"Are we going to sit here all night?" I whisper when his eyes focus on my mouth but he makes no move to get out of the truck.

"If we go inside—" he repeats.

"I know," I assure him once again.

"A lot has happened tonight. Your graduation party was ended abruptly because of the phone call Lawson got, and you—"

"I want to go inside with you."

He scrapes his hands down his face, refocusing on his front door. "Maybe we could—"

"If you don't want me inside—"

His groan is feral, the sound of a trapped beast demanding to be released.

"Inside is what I've wanted for the last two months."

My throat works on a swallow.

"Okay." I open my door and step out, waiting at the front of his truck for him to climb out.

He locks up the truck, stepping around me on the sidewalk. He doesn't touch me, doesn't brush my hip or press his hand to my back. I ache for his touch, ache for reassurance that he wasn't making empty promises just moments before.

With a trembling hand, he unlocks his front door, stepping away so I can enter first. Instead of sweeping me into his arms, he turns off the alarm system, flipping on lights as he walks deeper into his home.

"Colton?"

"Would you like something to drink?"

I watch him, his nerves on full display as he starts to pace.

"Are you nervous?" I aim for serious, but the question is laced with humor.

I don't think I've ever been moments away from stripping naked and the man I was getting naked for was turning shy.

"I wouldn't call it nerves."

I clasp his trembling hand.

"We can watch a movie—"

He huffs, his fingers tangling with mine. "I want to watch you come."

And those words light me up from the inside.

"Yeah?"

His teeth dig into his bottom lip. "I want your legs shaking. I want my name on your lips. I want to be inside of you so deep, you feel me in your soul."

How can I tell him he's already there?

"And you want that right here in the entryway?"

"My bed. I need you in my bed."

I squeal with delight when he scoops me up in his arms.

His lips are on mine, his tongue seeking, searching, licking my consent right out of my mouth.

Our hands are a blur, my dress hitting the soft carpet with a whisper the second we step inside his bedroom. The hiss of his zipper echoes around us, churning the atmosphere around us until we're both frenzied.

"Let me." He reaches behind me to unclasp my bra, the lace and satin tickling my skin as it falls away. "I'm one lucky man."

My cheeks heat, the anticipation of finally being with him, like this, is better than anything my mind could've conjured.

"You're beautiful when you blush." His fingers sweep over my face, trailing down my neck before tracing the curve of my collarbone.

"You're still dressed," I pout, my fingers inching toward his open fly.

He steps away, a mischievous look in his eyes. "And you're not completely naked."

His eyes flare when I dip my thumbs into the side of my panties and work them down my thighs. I know the second he sees the evidence of my desire. His eyelids lower, the pink tip of his tongue licking at the curve of his bottom lip. His reactions to me are the best aphrodisiac, making me want him more than I've ever wanted someone in my life.

"Now I am," I tease, standing there trying to look like a goddess when in fact I have no idea what to do with my hands.

When I lift them to my breasts, teasing the points of my nipples, I know I made the right choice. "Are you hard for me?"

In answer, he fists his cock, his hand sliding behind the open zipper of his jeans to grip it over the dark fabric of his briefs.

"So fucking hard. I need you in my mouth."

"This?" I cup the bottom swell of my right breast and hold it up as if I'm offering it to him.

He's not disappointed, his eyes zooming in on my hand.

"All of it." His eyes sweep my body. "Get on my bed, Sophia. I want your scent all over it."

I back away slowly, not willing to take my eyes off of him for a second. When his comforter brushes my thighs, I place my hands behind me and inch my way to the center of his bed.

"No," I tell him when he moves to climb on. "No clothes in this bed."

His grin is magnetic, and mine falls away when his shirt drops to the floor. I'm salivating when he shoves his jeans down. By the time his boxer briefs disappear, I'm breathless, panting in an attempt to pull enough oxygen in my lungs to function.

"I—shit—you're gorgeous."

His thick cock bobs freely as he moves, and I don't know where to focus as my eyes dart from his muscular thighs to the ridges lining his torso. His pecs flex as he climbs on the bed, but his mouth is a tempting focal point as well.

"Are you still with me?"

"I'm right here."

"You seem distracted."

"I am," I confess. "You're a lot to take in."

"So complimentary," he teases, his nose tracing the curve of my calf. "I'm distracted, too."

"Mmm."

"Where do you want my mouth?" He punctuates his question with a nip to my inner thigh.

"All over."

"Here?" His mouth teases my hip.

I nod, unable to form words. For a flash of a second, I feel like I should be embarrassed with how turned on I am. I know he can see my arousal. There's no way to hide the way my body is responding to him, preparing for him. Have I ever been this turned on in my life? That would be a no, and God, does this man make me want to do this every damn day of my existence.

"What about here?" His lips tickle the flesh just below my belly button.

"Lower," I pant, feeling his lips turn up into a smile against my overly sensitive skin.

"Here?" His breath ghosts over where I need him the most, his mouth once again on my inner thigh.

"Is this how you want to play it?"

His eyes meet mine, mouth still on my leg.

"I want to savor you. I want to spend the entire night worshipping your body."

"I want your mouth on my pussy," I counter, loving the way his eyes flare with my filthy declaration.

Perfect teeth dig into his bottom lip once again, and I can tell he's trying to hide a smile. It pulls one from my own mouth.

"But savor away," I tell him as my fingers trace over my breast, inching lower. His eyes find mine when I circle my belly button and aim lower. "Don't mind me."

His head pulls back mere inches as my wandering fingers skate over my clit. It takes sheer determination not to buck my hips with the first brush over it.

"Jesus, look at you." He gasps when I dip my fingers into my arousal before teasing my clit once again.

I'm seconds away from coming, a blink away from screwing my eyes tight and moaning with release.

"Does it feel good?"

"So good. You'd feel better."

"My fingers? Or my—"

His mouth is on me, his tongue tangling with the tips of my fingers, and I'm lost in him. Lost in the sensation of his heated mouth. Lost in the perfection of finally having him like this.

I'm just lost. My hand falls away, but doesn't stay near my hip for long. When he groans against me, my back bows, arching off the bed to the point of pain. Strong arms hold me against his mouth, and as I come, he laps at me, the incessant movement of his tongue making me tremble and flutter like I've never done before.

I chant his name until my throat is raw, and only after I seize a final time does he back away. Wetness coats his mouth and chin, and the grin on his face is reminiscent of a man who has just gotten everything he's ever wanted.

My eyes burn, the threat of tears making it impossible to speak.

"You're amazing."

I nod like a fool, hoping he understands that I think the same of him.

"I don't know what to do with you."

Love me forever.

I don't speak the words, but it's exactly what I want from him.

I want his love and affection. I want to wake each morning in his arms. I want to spend Saturday afternoons arguing about what to watch on television. I want to spend early mornings making love as the sun comes up.

"My turn," I finally manage after long moments of looking into each other's eyes.

He must be distracted because it takes minimal effort to get him on his back with his head against the headboard.

"Not gonna happen, gorgeous." His hands cling to my shoulders when I start to lower my mouth to the trail of hair below his navel.

"I want to return the favor."

"No."

My head snaps back, unsure of the direction he's taking.

"I want your cock in my mouth."

"And I want the first time I come with you to be deep inside your pussy." He angles his head to the side table. "Grab a condom."

His patience is commendable as I lean to the side to grab the unopened box of condoms from the drawer. My hands shake as I open it, trembling comically as I tear one from the strip. His hands trace the outer curve of my hips, making me insane with need.

"Let me," he says with his hand out, palm up.

I don't give him the condom once I have the wrapper removed. If he thinks he has the upper hand here, he's mistaken.

His teeth dig into his bottom lip when I touch him the first time, my free hand sliding down the length of him. He moans in need, and if I weren't straddling his thighs, I might have missed the way his muscles tighten under me.

"Deep breaths," I taunt as I tease the sensitive spot under his cockhead.

"Sophia," he warns when my thumb swirls in his precum. "Put the condom on, or I'm going to flip you over and fuck you bare."

He groans again when my thighs clench at the threat. We need a very long discussion before we get to that point, but it's a tantalizing offer either way.

More for my own mercy than his, I roll the condom down the length of him. His mouth is parted, breath slow and purposeful as I lift up on my knees and position him at my entrance.

We've both waited for this moment, but as much as I want to revel in it, my body demands more.

"Yes," he hisses, his fingers gripping my hips as I slide down. His body rolls under me, and we're both equally giving and taking at this moment. "Perfection."

"That sounds," I moan as I lift my weight and lower again, "so sexy."

"That sound means I'm not going to last," he warns. "That sound—God, you feel so fucking good."

"I knew," I gasp. "How did I know it would feel this good?"

Soon, talking isn't possible. Soon, my legs are shaking so hard, I can no longer get my legs to work. Soon, I'm trembling harder than I did the first time, my body convulsing around him in appreciation.

And soon, he's following me over the edge like he'd been waiting for me to whisper his name.

Chapter 25

Colton

I wake when the first hint of morning makes itself known, and a dozen things come into focus. I could focus on the warmth of her body against mine, or the softness of her hair brushing my arm. I could fixate on the way she let me keep my arms wrapped around her all night, or the way she has stayed slick between her milky thighs even after we fell to the mattress drained of energy from hours of fixating on each other.

But it's the soft snores that make me smile.

That and the erection that's been pressed against her ass for the last ten minutes. It only takes a few seconds for my fingers to brush the strip of condoms we stashed under the pillow and work it over my tired cock. I'm drained. We're both probably dehydrated, but you wouldn't be able to convince my lower half that we need a break.

My fingers find her wet as I split her folds and explore. The snores stop, replaced with a groan of pleasure, and it's all the permission I need to lift her thigh and position myself. Just like every time last night, sliding inside of her is a heaven I never thought I'd experience. Experiencing it over and over? I must have some very good karma saved up because never in my wildest dreams…

"You awake?" I whisper in her ear, my hips moving back and forth.

"Mmm," is her only response.

Well, that isn't entirely true. She lifts her leg, moving it back and over the top of mine, opening herself up in the most delicious way. My fingers tease her, skirting around her clit without actually touching it. I know if I do, she'll come, and even though that's the end goal, feeling her clench around me will set me off like a choreographed explosion, and I want to relish in the experience just a few moments longer.

"Feel good?"

"Always," she pants. "So good."

I've always considered sex functional, a quick way to release endorphins and better my mood, but with her, it's a whole event. It's not entirely about the outcome. I don't want inside of her just to get off. Our orgasms are the culmination, but not necessarily the main focus.

"Jesus, baby. Roll your hips."

She responds by gripping the arm I have wrapped around her, arching her back, and swiveling her perfect hips. She whimpers as she fucks herself on my cock, and I try my best not to mark her skin with fingertip-sized bruises.

"My clit," she begs. "Make me come."

Fuck, I thought she'd never ask.

I reposition our bodies with her stomach flat on the mattress and me behind her. I slam into her, sawing back and forth when I really want to take things slowly as my fingers make maddening circles on her clit.

"Higher," I urge, my hand smacking the globe of her ass, and her back arches like she was made to take me this way.

She screams my name, and I know I'll hear the echo of it every night when I close my eyes.

I grunt my release at the first whisper of her body rippling around mine, and my fingers don't stop moving between her legs until she squeals and pulls away.

"Join me in the shower?" I press my lips to her back, planting kisses along her spine.

"Hot water," she instructs as I climb off the bed.

I spend a few lingering minutes just watching her before turning around to do her bidding. The water scalds my skin, but she never joins me, and I'm not surprised to find her snoring gently when I walk back into my bedroom with water droplets still on my skin and a towel tight around my waist.

The sight of her naked, collapsed exactly where I left her before the shower is enough to rejuvenate my dick, but we both need a break and some breakfast. After throwing on some sweats and a t-shirt, I press my lips to her shoulder blade before covering her body with the comforter.

"I'm telling you, man, she's the hottest girl I've ever seen."

"I believe you."

"Tits like you've never seen."

"Really, Rick? And just how many sets of tits have you seen?"

I stop near the threshold to the living room. I swear teenage boys have a one-track mind.

An uneasy laugh slips from my son, but he doesn't answer the question.

"Exactly, and quit talking like that, dude. It's seriously fucking disrespectful."

I recognize Landon Andrew's voice, and I knew I liked this kid for a reason.

"Seriously?" Rick continues. "You stare at every female you pass."

"I'm trying to do better," Landon mutters.

"Sounds like you've had another conversation with your dad."

I narrow my eyes at this. After knowing what I know about the Cerberus MC, it's clear those men have raised good kids, but teen boys are a different breed. What they say and do in front of parents and how they act when they think no one is looking can be two different things.

"I had a... reaction."

"A reaction?" Rick questions. "Like a rash or something?"

A slap rings out. "No, you idiot. Like at the pool. I got hard."

"How hard?" I tilt my head to hear better.

"Quit looking at my crotch, fucker."

Rick laughs.

"I'll just say it was noticeable. People noticed. It was embarrassing."

"I imagine."

"So when are you going to talk about the argument you had with Seth?"

"I'm not fucking talking about it," Rick hisses.

My stomach grumbling reminds me why I left Sophia alone in my bed, so I cough to make myself known before walking out of the hallway.

"Hey, Dad," Rick mumbles.

"Hey, Mr. Matthews."

"Colton," I remind the kid with a quick grin. Most kids pretend to be respectful in the face of adults, but after listening in to part of their conversation, it's clear this young man is being genuine.

The boys are sitting on either sides of the couch. The television is on, volume low.

"You guys hungry? I was gonna make breakfast."

"For us, or your friend?"

"Are you hungry or not?" I repeat as I turn in the direction of the kitchen.

Rick either isn't aware of Landon and Sophia's connection or he doesn't care. I don't think her being here at the same time as Landon is a big deal, but her coming out with no warning wouldn't be fair to either of them. I have no clue how she wants to handle this situation even though I know last night and this morning wasn't a fluke. She's going to be spending more time here, and Landon comes over often enough that their paths are eventually going to cross. First thing on a Saturday morning without knowing exactly what the boys heard from my room earlier probably isn't the perfect time though.

"Pancakes and eggs?" I ask as I open the fridge.

I know I have an awkward conversation coming with Dominic, but with any luck, I won't have to have it today.

"You don't have to cook for us Mr. Matt—Colton."

"He doesn't speak for me," Rick says with a smile as he slides past to get into the fridge. "What about bacon?"

He places the unopened package of meat near the stove before taking a long swig of orange juice from the container.

"Get a glass, you heathen," I chide, but all he does is smile and take another drink.

"Juice?" he asks his friend when there's only a little left in the jug.

"No way, man. I'm not getting anywhere near where your mouth has been."

Rick shrugs before polishing off the juice.

I make quick work of the food, insisting they take their plates to Rick's room to eat.

"Is it because you don't want your girlfriend checking me out again?" Rick says as he reaches for his plate.

"Go, Rick."

"Maybe next time keep it down. I didn't get a wink of sleep last night. You know a growing boy needs his sleep."

Landon's cheeks flush, and he avoids eye contact with me. It makes me wonder if he has ever had conversations with his parents like this.

Rick is cackling like a lunatic as he walks out of the room.

Landon stumbles on the threshold, plate in hand. "He's joking. We stayed at Aaron's house last night."

The redness in his face as he walks away tells me that they were here long enough to bear audible witness to what Sophia and I did this morning.

And that's another consideration we need to discuss. Having an active sex life is healthy, and I plan to spend as much time inside of her as she allows, but we have to keep in mind that Rick and his friends could be lurking around at any moment.

I'm pouring coffee into two mugs on a tray when Sophia walks into the room. Her hair is a mess, face marked with lines from the pillow, but it's her soft knowing smile that makes everything come into focus.

"I was bringing you breakfast," I say softly as she walks to me, pressing her chest against my body.

Without hesitation, I place the coffee pot back on the machine and wrap my arms around her.

This is how it should've been that first night she was here, and I want to kick myself for not doing this sooner. I press my nose into her hair, inhaling the scent of the two of us.

My cock, although exhausted from the time we've spent together, jerks in my sweats. She chuckles like it's exactly what she expected, but she doesn't make a move to take things further. I'm equal parts relieved and flustered.

"Can't get enough of you," I confess, my face still buried in her hair.

"Want to join me in the shower?"

"Need me to wash your back?" I tease.

"Yeah." Her fingers slide under my shirt, and I never thought the brush of fingers on my spine could be sexual, but here we are. "I'm feeling extra dirty this morning."

I hold her tighter, imagining what my cum would look like striped across her tits, mixing with soap suds.

"What about breakfast?"

"I'm not—"

Her stomach loudly interrupts, grumbling its displeasure.

"I made pancakes, eggs, and bacon."

"Are you trying to spoil me?"

"Is it working?"

"I don't think I ever want to leave."

Her fingers dig in deeper, emphasizing her confession.

"Mmm," I groan against the top of her head. Her hair tickles my nose, but it's not enough of an irritation to make me release my hold on her. "I like the sound of that."

"Is breakfast in bed still an option?"

"If we take this to my room, I don't know that pancakes are still going to be on the menu."

"I thought you wanted to eat," she says as she takes a step back.

My eyes burn into hers. "Oh, I'll be eating if we go back to bed."

White teeth dig into her lower lip, and I can see she's weighing the possibilities. I might have to gag her to keep her quiet, but going the rest of the day without being inside of her again, even with the boys here isn't an option.

That reminds me...

"Rick isn't alone this morning. He brought—"

As if thoughts of him caused him to appear, Sophia turns around and comes face-to-face with Landon.

Well, shit.

Chapter 26

Sophia

I never understood what people really meant when they said they were frozen in place. I grew up with a dad whose number one favorite thing was interrogating his daughters. I learned from an early age to at least attempt to talk my way out of trouble, but seeing Dustin and Khloe's son standing in Colton's kitchen, all I can manage is staring at him, praying with each blink of my eyes that he disappears.

At least I'm not half-naked like I was the first time I met Colton's parents, but the mop on my head and the ill-fitting clothes I grabbed out of Colton's drawer are as good as any flashing sign of what I've been up to.

I don't know what to say, but starting a conversation with *when two adult people love each other* doesn't seem like the best idea either. First off, I haven't even had that conversation with Colton and second, there's really nothing I can say that won't make it back to the clubhouse in the next damn hour.

Landon doesn't look surprised to see me here, and it makes me wonder how many conversations Rick has had with him about me.

"Morning," I say stupidly as all three of us stare at each other.

"Morning," Landon replies, a small smile tugging up the corners of his mouth as he looks between Colton and me.

I can already see his mind working on ways to blackmail me with this newly discovered situation.

"This isn't—"

"This is exactly what it looks like," I counter, not wanting to make things worse with Colton trying to lie for us.

We're adults, and we can both do what we want with each other without having to worry about the sensibilities of a boy whose eyes bug out of his head anytime a female walks by. If he wants to make a bigger deal out of this than it is, I'll just bring up what a couple of the girls were talking about last night at the graduation party. Apparently, being a teenage boy and unable to control yourself in public is a very hard and embarrassing thing to struggle with.

"I didn't—"

I hold my hand up to stop Landon, and his jaw snaps closed. "Can I speak with Landon alone?"

Colton looks down at me, unease filling his dark blue eyes, and I have no idea what he's worried about. It isn't like Landon is going to hurt me or try to blackmail me, even though I'm not above offering him cold hard cash to keep his adolescent mouth closed until I'm ready to disclose this situation to my parents and every other person at the clubhouse. Lord knows once the match is lit, the information will blaze through there like flames kissing the edge of a dry field.

"Are you sure?" Colton looks at me like Landon doesn't exist, and I love that he's concerned for me.

"I'll be fine. Just need to have a little chat with my buddy." Colton nods before backing away, and until the cool air of the kitchen hits my back, I don't realize he's been plastered against me this whole time. "Don't forget the food. I know how hungry you get."

Colton snorts before wrapping his big hands around the handles of the tray and walking out of the room.

"Crazy seeing you here," Landon says after Colton's bedroom door closes.

"Don't start with me."

"What would Dominic say?" He winks. "Didn't know you had a thing for older men."

"He's not that much older than me," I argue.

"You're closer in age to Ricky than you are Colton."

I narrow my eyes at him as he crosses his arms over his chest and leans against the doorframe. What is it about men in this house doing that?

"Rick is a child. Colton isn't. So your reasoning doesn't make sense."

"I see." He nods his head as if he understands, but that little annoying smile is still on his face.

"What do you want?"

"What do you mean?"

"I guess you want something for your silence?"

His brow furrows.

"No."

"And is this you playing hardball?"

"What?"

"What. Do. You. Want?"

"For what?"

"In exchange for your silence."

He stands, growing taller than I remember him being, but the action doesn't have an imposing feel to it.

"I don't want your money or favors."

I throw my hands in the air in irritation. "Then what?"

"Nothing, Sophia. I don't want anything."

"Because nothing will keep you from running back to the clubhouse to blab?"

"Blab? I'm not a fuc—" His mouth snaps closed. "I'm not a kid. I'm not going to run off and tattle on you."

"Because you expect the same courtesy if I see you doing something wrong?"

"Who hurt you?"

"What?" The question makes me take a step back, only the counter is there, and I don't remember moving since we started talking.

"I'm not going to blackmail you. I'm not going to expect anything for my silence. This isn't my business."

"Really?" Surely he isn't that damn mature. He's only sixteen, and teens are notoriously looking for a way to benefit from every situation.

"Really. Do you know how many weekends I'm over here?"

"I have no clue." I cross my own arms over my chest because I'm feeling oddly vulnerable right now. There are a million things I don't know about Colton, and it chafes a little that this kid may know more than I do.

"A lot," he clarifies. "Not once have I walked in here and seen a smile so big on Colton's face, or a morning where he isn't shuffling to get out the door to go to work."

"Really?"

"He comes out of his room with a wide smile on his face, relaxed in sweats, and I tell you what, it looks good on him. If you're the reason he's different this morning, then I say more power to the two of you. He's an incredible man. He's an awesome dad. Rick, although he doesn't know when to shut his mouth sometimes, is one of my best friends. He's someone Mom and Dad approve of because he was raised the way we were. Do you know how hard that is to find these days? And that man raised him alone. That in itself shows his character. You could do worse than Colton Matthews."

"So you were just giving me shit about our age difference?"

Landon shrugs, and it seems like an incredibly simple action with the mature words that just came out of his mouth. "You're both adults."

"We are," I confirm.

"Do you love him?"

Jesus, talk about coming out with the big guns.

"Because I don't think he's going to let you go. He's too much like Dad, too much like Dominic. I've never seen a woman over here, just like I've never seen him look at someone the way I saw him look at you. I sure as hell hope you're in it for the long haul, because it's clear that man is."

"How are you only sixteen?"

He grins at this. "You forget my birthday is in a few weeks. Seventeen and completely legal."

"Can't vote until you're eighteen," I remind him.

He winks at me. "Legal to consent."

I don't even try to stop the chuckle that escapes my throat. The boy thinks he's God's gift to women.

"Would it be weird if I asked you about Rick?"

"Depends."

"Do I need to worry about him, like hitting on me? I don't want to come between him and his dad, but I also don't want to be uncomfortable around here either."

I expect reassurance, a quick answer, but that isn't what I get. Landon looks away, thinking about my question for a long moment before answering.

"Rick is complicated, but I can guarantee he's a hundred percent talk. If he flirts, just ignore him and he'll stop. Pretty soon, you'll figure out that he only does it when he has an audience. He's a great guy, but he feels the need to put on a show."

"He'll grow out of it." That may actually be a lie because I've met dozens of guys—adults honestly—that have never grown out of peacocking for the benefit of others.

"Hopefully."

"So, we're good here? I don't have to worry about getting plowed over the next time I go to the clubhouse?"

"Your secret is safe with me," he says.

"It's not that it's a secret. We're going to tell people, but we just have to do it in our own time."

"And I understand needing to figure things out before opening a door that may never close again."

Sadness fills his eyes, but he turns away before I can question him.

"True," I agree.

"Just be careful."

"I don't think he'll break my heart."

His eyes find mine again, the sadness still there and heartbreaking. His phone chirps with a text, but he only glances at it before finding my eyes again.

"I'm not worried about your heart. It's different getting involved with a family than dating a single guy."

"I know." And I do. It's something that has always been a consideration since finding out about Rick.

"Okay," he whispers before walking away.

He doesn't head down the hall toward Rick's room. Instead, he walks out the front door, not even saying goodbye to his friend. I have to trust that he isn't going to run off and speak about what he saw today, but that assurance doesn't calm the feelings swimming around in my gut.

Colton isn't in his bedroom when I go look for him, but I find him and Rick with their heads bent together talking. I don't know what to do. Should I interrupt them? Walk away?

Maybe this is yet another conversation I need to have with Colton. So much is happening so fast, and it's becoming almost too much to deal with at one time. My feet urge me to the front door but taking off without explaining isn't the mature way to handle things. That's done with talking and uncomfortable discussions.

I fire off a text to Izzy, wondering what happened after I left the clubhouse. It doesn't take long for her to respond that her dad is livid.

Izzy: When I told him I was pregnant, I thought he was going to blow a gasket.

Me: He'll come around.

Izzy: Maybe, I'm not so sure. He left last night pissed off and hasn't come home.

Me: Maybe he's helping with the Drew situation?

I don't believe it as I type it. Whatever is going on with Drew would be handled with closed ranks, and as much as Hound is part of the Cerberus group, he's not in the core circle which includes my dad, Uncle Diego, Rob, Jaxon and Morrison, and Dustin–Landon's dad.

Izzy: Did you hear what happened?

Me: I haven't.

Is it selfish of me for spending time with Colton rather than sticking around to get the latest news on Drew? Suddenly, I feel like an irresponsible jerk.

Izzy: I only know what I read online because no one is talking, but from what I saw, Drew went apeshit on some guy at a scene and killed him.

I can sympathize with Drew because there have been times while I was working with Colton that I wanted to bloody my knuckles on someone who had no respect for human life.

Me: Wow.

Izzy: Yeah.

Me: Did you ever meet him?

I've only ever seen Drew two or three times in the last couple years, and one of those times was during his short stay with Jaxon and Rob before his paternal grandparents came for him. They moved him to New England and I think he's only been back once since.

Izzy: Nope.

I drop my phone when the bedroom door opens, and the look in Colton's eyes tell me that he's no longer in the mood for breakfast.

I don't feel that way either. There's too much going on, too many things between us that we need to hash out. The sex has been great, amazing even, but if we want this to work between us, we need to sit down and talk it all out.

"I—can I just hold you?"

I nod my agreement, needing his touch as much as it seems he needs mine.

Chapter 27

Colton

The entire day since Sophia left has been insanely weird.

She didn't talk much after Landon left, and I can't help but wonder if he said something that made her change her mind. She let me hold her in the bed but despite our physical closeness, I could feel her pulling away.

Does people knowing about us make her uneasy?

I want to call Dominic and tell him everything, but that seems like an incredibly selfish thing to do considering everything that family is going through right now. I know Sophia isn't related by blood to Lawson and his brother, but the MC is as close as I've ever seen a biological family.

Me: Missing you already.

She left mere hours ago but the time and miles of distance seems like an eternity and worlds apart.

Maybe it's the unknown that's making me question everything that's happened. My body doesn't regret a thing. The time we spent, the ways we came together could never be a mistake, but that isn't keeping my head from jumbling everything up.

"I thought you had plans," I tell Rick as he walks into the room, collapsing beside me on the sofa.

"Canceled," he huffs, eyes straight ahead on the news playing on television.

"I thought it would take a catastrophe to cancel a teenager's plans."

"Or someone being charged with murder."

That makes me pause.

"We stayed at Aaron's house last night. Landon just found out what was going on with one of the guys linked to the club."

"I see." How do I talk to my son about this?

As a detective, I'm inclined to lean toward commending the arresting officers for being strong enough to arrest one of their own, but my experience tells me that nothing is as black-and-white as most want to believe. There are always extenuating circumstances with every case.

"Do you have any details?"

"I was hoping you'd have some."

"I don't know much. Drew O'Neil works for the state police. He responded to a call and someone ended up dead. The state police are keeping things close to the chest right now."

"Murder?"

"Technically, it's only classified as a homicide right now. It hasn't even been twenty-four hours. There's a good chance he hasn't been formally charged yet."

"Sucks," he mutters, lifting his feet to the coffee table. "Everyone has been ordered to the clubhouse. It's like they're closing ranks or something."

"I imagine the situation is rocking everyone involved."

"Landon isn't involved, and if he's the type of guy to defend a bad cop, I don't know what to think about that."

"Drew's arrest doesn't necessarily make him a bad cop."

"If he wasn't guilty, he wouldn't have been arrested."

"That's not how it works, Rick."

I've never had long conversations with my son about my job. Not only does he seem disinterested in police work, I think he's a little scared to know full details about how dangerous it can actually be.

"The police arrest on probable cause. It's up to a judge and jury to decide guilt." I turn the volume on the television down all the way. "What we know is someone is dead and someone was arrested for it. We have to wait for more details before passing judgment."

"That's nearly impossible."

"It is," I agree.

"It sucks."

"It sucks that your plans were canceled or—"

"It sucks that my best friend is going through something, and I can't be there for him."

"I'm sorry your plans were canceled, but I'm actually glad you're here."

He groans, sinking further into the sofa. "Please tell me we aren't having a sex talk."

"Not exactly." I smile at his reluctance. "I do want to talk about Sophia."

His mouth turns up in a grin, but the smile doesn't reach his eyes. There are a lot of things I know this young man needs to speak with me about. Many, I won't push the issue on because I know those conversations need to happen at his own pace, but I can't let Sophia be a subject that festers.

"How do you feel about her spending more time over here?"

He shrugs.

"I need a real answer."

"She's smoking hot, Dad. It's not exactly a hardship to have her around."

I take a deep breath, holding it in my lungs before releasing it on a whoosh. I'm not agitated or frustrated, but it's clear he's deflecting. I just have to figure out which parts are causing him concern.

"I find her extremely attractive as well."

He snorts, his eyes still focused on the television even though I know he doesn't have an ounce of interest in the evening news.

"I'm going to be spending a lot of time with her." God willing. "I need you to tell me if you start feeling neglected."

He snorts again. "Neglected? Come on, Dad. I'm nearly seventeen. I'm not going to complain about less attention. If anything, I'm going to love it."

"And that's another thing I worry about."

"I'm responsible," he grumbles.

"I know."

We haven't exactly struggled as I raised him because my parents were always around to help, but I tried my best not to lean on them too much. I've never looked at Rick like a burden or a mistake. His arrival just catapulted me into adulthood quicker than I had planned.

"This is a new situation for all of us."

"I never told you not to date."

"But the fact remains that I haven't had anything serious with a woman in a very long time. It's as new for me as it is for you."

"You've been alone too long. I just want you to be happy."

Would he find it weird if I hugged him right now? I stay sitting with my ass firmly planted on the couch, not wanting to ruin the moment.

"I'm happy when I'm with her."

"I've noticed." He chuckles, eyeing me from the side.

"I want you to know I've never been unhappy. Raising you has been my primary focus all of these years. I honestly never thought I'd get a chance at being happy with someone romantically."

It's been no secret that love and true affection weren't in the cards where his mother was concerned. I've been as honest with him as his age and maturity level allowed when he had questions. My parents don't bad mouth her, but we never put her on a pedestal she didn't earn either.

"Sophia isn't my mom," he whispers, more pain in his voice than I think he even realizes.

I can't imagine growing up without a mother, and although we haven't talked much about her in recent years, I know he feels the loss of something he can never remember having. Landon's parents are still together. So are Aaron's. He seeks out friends that have two-parent households. I like to think he does that because he was also raised in a healthy environment, not that I believe for a second that a single-parent household has a negative impact. I've proven that it can be just as healthy, sometimes healthier than sharing a life with someone who doesn't want to be there.

His mother walking away from her responsibilities is a blessing I count daily. Some people aren't meant to stick around. I'm just glad she made that decision early on instead of after he was old enough to remember her.

"I know she isn't," I answer before I spend too much time getting lost in my own head. "And I don't think she has any aspirations of bossing you around."

"A hot stepmom? Sign me up." He winks at me, and all I can do is shake my head.

"And that mess needs to stop. I don't want her uncomfortable."

"Did she say something?" He finally looks at me, frowning as he waits for my answer. "I've just been joking."

"She hasn't, and I don't think it bothers her much, but maybe stop while you're ahead?"

"Sure thing," he agrees quickly. "Is she coming over tonight?"

I look down at my dark phone, knowing if I check it again, it's not going to magically make a text appear. She hasn't responded to my text from earlier, and I'm still wondering if I played too many cards too quickly.

"Not tonight, I don't think. She's part of those people that are circling the wagons right now just like Landon."

Our conversation begins to shift, going from Sophia to Rick's last couple of weeks in school. He's a bright kid, never having really struggled with school until the last two years. He claims to have been distracted but doesn't go into detail. He assures me he's going to pass all his classes without needing summer school like last year. I make sure before he gets off the couch to go to bed that he knows how proud I am of him.

He shrugs off the praise like he always has, like he's got secrets he believes will make me change my mind.

My heart is heavy and my bed is empty by the time I lock the house down and turn off all the lights. Only the soft thump of music coming from Rick's room can be heard as I close myself in my own bedroom.

Waking up high on a cloud and going to bed filled with the unknown is draining. I check my phone one last time before lying down, deciding it's best to send her a final text telling her goodnight.

That one goes unanswered too.

Chapter 28

Sophia

A quiet house has never bothered me. A quiet clubhouse is a whole other story.

Half the team, including my mom and dad are in Albuquerque dealing with the Drew situation, and the other half of the team have a job in South America. Tensions are always high when Cerberus is out of town on a mission, but the atmosphere for most of the day before they departed was rife with stress no one was openly speaking about.

Those of us left behind know there's a lot going on, but no one seemed willing to talk about it. I learned as a child not to ask many questions, not that they would've been answered, and even as an adult, I'm left in the dark more often than not.

Izzy and I have taken up residence in the only room left empty, but even her soft breaths as she sleeps don't calm my nerves.

The text messages Colton sent draw all of my attention even with my phone dark and on the bedside table. He misses me, and I miss him, but listening to Landon tell me to be careful with him and Rick hit me in the chest like a tanker truck.

I want to think I'm doing the right thing, but I haven't stuck with anything in my life long-term except for school, and had I gotten bored, I don't know that I would've graduated.

Opening my life up to Colton means also opening up to Rick. They're a package deal, something I didn't know in the beginning when I let myself fantasize about an older man. I'm not uneasy with him having a son. You can't really expect someone to have no history, but it's the future I'm worried about.

Can I love a man who loves someone so fiercely? Would my love even compare to that or his love for me?

I'm selfish. I know that. I'm fickle. I can admit to that as well, but those two traits have no business in a relationship with a man with a child, no matter how nearly grown the young man is.

Rick will always come first, and I know that's how it should be. What I can't stop asking myself is if I'll be okay with that. Will I be okay with being the second choice? What if Rick and I don't agree on something? Will Colton side with him because it's his son, even if he's wrong?

I have a million questions, but the one thing that's keeping my eyes wide open when I should be sleeping is knowing that no matter the answers to any of them, I've fallen for that man. I can't see myself carrying on with my life without him being there with me. I don't want to walk away not knowing the kind of future we should have.

Mom always told me loving a kid was different from loving others when I asked her how she had enough love for me when she would've given all of her love to Jasmine, who is technically her half-sister. At the time, she told me something about her heart growing to hold more love, and I remember watching her as she smiled at me, Jasmine or my dad, waiting to see her chest open up to accommodate all the love that was filling her because it was always on her face, in her words, and in her actions.

As I got older, I understood what she was talking about, and how that love wasn't a physical thing, but an ability to love many people that came into my life without sacrificing those feelings for others.

Like getting hit by a lightning bolt, I sit straight up in bed. Colton could love me as much as he loves his son. It's a different love, a different spot in his chest, and I know there's room there. I love many people, and I know there's a whole section of my soul that belongs to him.

With shaking hands, I scoop up my phone, shove my feet into my sandals, and walk out of the room. I'm met with eerie silence in the living room of the clubhouse, but determination keeps my feet moving. The drive to Colton's house seems to take forever despite the fact that it's the middle of the night and hardly anyone is driving around.

The power driving me across town leaves me anxious when I pull into his driveway. All the doubts I had earlier come crashing back. I'm able to get out of the car and to his front door by sheer will alone. My feet tell me to turn and run, that if I leave now, I'll be safe. If I leave now, I won't risk my heart getting broken, I won't somehow break Colton's or Rick's heart.

My eyes are burning, tears threatening to fall when I lift my hand and knock. I know my knuckle doesn't hit the wood hard enough to wake anyone, and I think that's another subconscious way for me to say I was here and tried without actually facing him.

Then the damn door opens.

Colton stands in front of me, hair ruffled, sleep in his eyes, and his gun held down at his side.

"Soph? What are you doing here?"

He takes a step back, disappearing inside before coming back to the door empty-handed.

"Expecting trouble?" I tease, but there's no humor in my voice.

"You're trouble," he whispers, his eyes a little glazed and focused on my lips.

It would be so easy to step into him, let him make me forget about all the things I've been worried about, but the problems wouldn't disappear though. My concern would be just as viable tomorrow as they are right now. Going inside, getting another taste of him, another night in his arms will only make things worse if we don't work out. I feel a little manic standing here. My legs want to move, but at the same time, I'm rooted in place. I want to wrap my arms around him, but they hang heavily at my sides.

The tears I thought I'd be strong enough to keep from falling have begun to crest my lashes and are rolling down my cheeks.

"Please," he says, and I don't know what he wants.

The pain on his faces makes my heart clench in my chest.

"Please don't do this to me." Anguish distorts his handsome face as he takes a step back, much of his profile lost in the shadows.

"I don't know how to explain what I'm feeling." I lick at the tears flowing over my lips. "It's a crushing weight, but at the same time when I'm with you, I feel free."

I have to concentrate not to lower my eyes to my hands even though I want to look away from him. I feel more exposed than I ever have, and instinct tells me to hide.

"Is it love? Do I love you?"

He clears his throat but doesn't speak.

"Is that selfish? I don't want to hurt you or Rick. Is wanting you selfish? It would probably be easier to walk away."

"I'd be devastated if you did." He takes a step closer, his handsome blue eyes darting between mine.

"Why?" I manage.

"Because I love you, too."

"I'm terrified of what that means," I confess.

"Me too."

I want his hands on me. I want to be in his arms. I want the assurance that whatever life throws at us, we'll make it because we're stronger when we're side by side.

"You love me?" I ask, because I'll never get tired of hearing it.

"I love you."

Tingles cover every inch of my skin as butterflies take flight in my stomach.

Was all the worry for nothing? I have no doubt we'll hit snags as we traverse our new relationship, but can happiness really come this easily?

"Are you going to stand out there all night?" he asks, a glint of devious intent in his eyes.

"Is Rick home?"

"He is, but you're welcome here any time."

"I don't want to make things weird for your son."

"We spent the better part of the evening discussing you."

"And you still want me in your home?" I chuckle, trying to add some humor, but he doesn't laugh at my half attempt at a joke.

"I love you, Sophia." *Will I ever get tired of hearing him say that?* "Of course I talked with Rick. He's a part of my life, and I wanted to make sure he was aware that you're going to be a part of it too."

"He's okay with me being here?"

"More than okay. Do I have to pick you up and carry you? My bed is calling my name."

"Tired?"

He doesn't answer, and when I squeal when he steps close and picks me up, I know I've probably awoken the neighbors.

"Am I going to have to gag you?" he asks as he urges my legs around his waist so he can carry me inside.

I can't answer him because our lips crash together. With me still in his arms, he locks the front door, grabs his firearm and walks us in the direction of his room.

"Can't wait to get you naked," I breathe against his lips, his cock already thickening against my center.

"Ah! Gross. Get a room."

I stiffen at the sound of Rick at my back.

"And maybe keep the squealing to a minimum?"

Colton laughs, his head buried in my throat as Rick closes his bedroom door. Music, louder than decent at this time of night, filters out, and for a split second I feel sorry for the kid. My parents are very affectionate with each other, and I remember nights when my skin would crawl, knowing what they were doing in their room because they were being too loud.

"I'm going to buy him noise canceling headphones," I vow as Colton carries us into his room.

"He has them, but I'm sure he would appreciate the gesture."

I bounce on the bed with a squeal, covering my mouth and eyeing the front wall of the room. Rick's bedroom is across the hall, and I don't think I've even been happier about one room not sharing a wall with another in my life.

Colton deposits his gun in the bedside drawer before turning his attention back to me.

"Maybe we should just cuddle," I offer, even though my body is humming with need.

Being a responsible adult in charge of others means sometimes forfeiting what you want for what's appropriate.

"Not a fucking chance," Colton says as he shoves his sweats down his legs.

How have I only now noticed that he answered the door without a shirt? Dark chest hair calls to me, and I want to feel the soft brush of it on my lips. I didn't get enough of it last night. I don't know that I'll ever get enough of it.

"Get naked," he insists, but I watch distracted as he produces a condom and rolls it down his very eager and ready cock.

"He'll hear us," I argue, but my hands are already working open the buttons on my jeans.

"We'll be quiet."

Apparently, I'm not moving fast enough because he climbs on the bed with me, removing my shirt and staring down in awe at my tits.

"No bra?"

"I was in bed when I decided to come here," I explain, my needy fingers getting tangled in my panties in my bid to shove them down my legs.

Being the helpful guy that he is, Colton lowers his body, using his mouth to get them free.

"Oh God!" I hiss when he licks up my center on the way back up my body.

"That gag is sounding like a good idea."

"Your fault," I pant when he presses his hands into the mattress near my head and leans in to kiss me. "Shouldn't feel so good."

"I'll never touch you without bringing you pleasure."

"I can't be quiet," I warn as he lines himself up with an expert swivel of his hips.

"I'll go slow," he promises, but even as he fills me inch by slow delicate inch, I moan his name loud enough to wake the dead.

Chapter 29

Colton

"Are you sure you don't need more cheese?"

Sophia flips me the bird over her shoulder before grabbing another handful of cheese and sprinkling it over the omelet she's cooking.

Seeing her in my kitchen, although wearing more clothes than I'd like, is like a dream come true.

My throat still wants to seize at the memory of why I thought she showed up last night, and I know I'm one lucky motherfucker for it to turn into a confession of love rather than her ripping my heart out on my front porch at two in the morning.

"Eventually, you're going to have to worry about cholesterol," I warn with a smile on my face.

"Don't listen to the old man," Rick says on a yawn as he enters the room. "Not everyone is going to end up on Lipitor."

Sophia chuckles, tossing Rick a quick smile before turning back to the stove.

"Want an omelet?" she asks as she plates the one she's working on. I grin at her as she hands me the cheesy dish. "How's your life insurance?"

"Trying to get rid of me already?"

Rick watches us, his head volleying back and forth as we banter.

"Death by eggs?"

"Death by cheese," I tell her with a wink, pressing my lips to her cheek before she can step away.

I take a deliberate bite before pretending to choke and grabbing at my heart.

"Adults are weird," Rick mutters as he reaches in the fridge. "We're out of juice."

"You guzzled it all yesterday," I remind him. "It's on the list. I'll grab some this evening."

Knowing I'll forget, Rick pulls the magnetic marker from the fridge and jots it down on the list.

"Omelet?" Sophia asks again.

"Whole eggs or egg whites?"

"Whole. Unless you only want whites."

"Whole is fine," Rick says with a grin, and I already know where this is going. I didn't figure he'd test her so early on, but I guess he wouldn't be my kid if he didn't break someone in right out of the gate. "But can you dice my meat smaller? Is that ham? I prefer turkey and tiny crumbles of bacon. And make sure it only has an ounce and a half of bell peppers, and a teaspoon of onion because I don't want bad breath all day. Also, can you pick all the Colby out of that cheese blend? It doesn't fit my macros."

Sophia doesn't even look at me, her eyes darting between my son and the ingredients on the counter.

"I can leave something in or take something out. If you want to measure everything out to your specifications, I'll be happy to toss that mess in the pan when you're done."

With a hand on her hip, she watches him, waiting for his answer.

"Loads of meat, no veggies. As much cheese as you can add in."

She narrows her eyes, waiting to see if it's another test.

"Perfect," she says after a long beat.

When she turns back to the stove, he gives me a thumbs up as he walks closer.

I grin at his antics.

"Why is she cooking?" he whispers as he takes a seat at the kitchen bar to my right.

"She wanted to."

"That looks incredible." He motions his head toward my plate. "Can I have a bite?"

"No," I hiss, smacking his hand with the back of my fork when he reaches for a piece of bacon on my plate. "Wait for your own."

"She's going to spit in my food after what I just did."

"She won't," I promise, but we both keep a vigilant eye on her until she hands over his plate.

He finishes his before she can get the eggs cracked for her own.

We don't speak as we watch her cooking in our kitchen.

"You're happy," he says, breaking the silence.

"Extremely," I confirm.

"I don't mean to ruin your day." He looks up at Sophia as she sets her plate on the bar across from where we're sitting. "I imagine Sophia will be joining us for dinner?"

I tense as I watch her reaction, but since she's uninformed what Rick is talking about, she simply grins at him.

"Do you have special instructions? Maybe you want spaghetti but only with pureed sauce, and let me guess, can I pick out all the parsley because anything green doesn't fit in your macros?" She smiles around a cheesy bite of omelet.

"No. You don't have to worry about cooking anything. My grandmother prepares the entire meal."

Her eyes find mine, and she begins to choke.

I glare at my son as I rush around the bar and clap her on the back.

"You okay?" I ask when she's finally drawing in ragged breaths, and I'm certain she doesn't need the Heimlich maneuver.

"D-Dinner?" she sputters. "With your parents?"

"We go every Sunday when Dad isn't working," Rick says with an innocent smile. "They've been expecting you to show up with us for weeks."

Sophia's head swivels on her shoulders until she's glaring at me.

"What?" I back away, wondering if now would be the time to call in a priest for an exorcist. "You were here when they invited you the first time."

"I thought they were just being polite."

"My mother would never invite someone to sit down at her table if she didn't want them there."

"They saw me in your shirt," she whisper-hisses. "I was half-naked in this very kitchen. I thought they didn't want to seem rude."

Rick laughs, making the situation worse.

"I figured they invited all the women they've caught you with."

"They haven't—"

"Dad doesn't have women over." He smiles widely. "You're the first."

"The only," I clarify. "I don't bring women home."

"You only brought me home because I was drunk."

"Rick, can you go to your room?"

"I thought this was a family discussion." I could strangle this damn boy.

"You weren't drunk last night, and yet here you are," I remind her, my voice growing low, intent clear in my eyes.

What started as a mild shock about an invitation to dinner is somehow transforming into a situation that's going to turn graphic very soon.

Rick clears his throat, giving us both a wide berth as he places his plate in the sink. He thanks Sophia for breakfast before hauling ass out of the kitchen.

"You don't look like you want to discuss dinner any longer."

"Was that the goal? You know I like it when you argue with me."

"You do?"

Okay, maybe she didn't know, but the tent in my sweats is physical proof of my words.

"Are you saying you don't want to join us? I'm not going to force you, but I'd like to have you there."

"You don't think that's moving too fast?"

"They wanted you there weeks ago. I wanted you there weeks ago. Things aren't moving fast enough if you ask me."

"Really?"

"My parents were very impressed with you."

"They spent less than an hour with me, and they grilled me the entire time."

"The inquisition will only continue if you join us this evening."

"Are you trying to deter me from going?"

"I don't want you blindsided."

"Don't you think it's weird? You haven't met my parents."

"I met your parents at the grocery store the night I cornered you at the bar."

My cock thickens even further at the memory of being pressed against her, my drunken confessions slipping past loose lips.

"You don't think it will be weird?"

"It's been weird for weeks," I tell her truthfully. "They ask about you every Sunday. Mom won't shut up about it."

"I'd like to go, if you're okay with it."

"I want you there," I whisper against her lips, my fingers tangling in the oversized t-shirt of mine she insisted on wearing before we left my room earlier.

"I don't have anything to wear. I'll need to go home to change."

"You can wear what you have on."

"Not funny." She smacks my chest her hand lingering over my heart.

"It wouldn't be the first time they saw you in my clothes."

She tweaks my nipple, finding it shockingly quickly over my own shirt.

I hiss in pain but don't release her. "Too soon?"

"Are you sure they don't want me over there just to try to run me off?"

"I'm certain. They wouldn't tell me they liked you if they didn't. My parents aren't fake people. They speak their minds, and this time when talking about you, it was something I needed to listen to."

"Are you telling me your parents helped you decide to be with me?"

"They encouraged it, but I knew it was inevitable. Walking away while loving you wasn't ever going to happen."

"Is that so?"

She grins, her gorgeous eyes sparkling the way they have every time I've confessed my feelings for her.

"I'm going to be a nervous wreck."

"I know a way to solve that problem before we even leave the house."

With my words, she takes several steps back, making my arms fall to my sides.

"Nope."

"What do you mean, nope?"

She holds her hands up when I reach for her again. I look around the room, making sure my son isn't creeping around since teens are so damn light on their feet these days.

"I know the perfect way to relax you before spending several hours with my parents."

"Is it yoga?" I shake my head as she backs further away from me. "Is it a nap?"

"It's orgasms," I offer, instead of her wasting another minute with ridiculous guesses.

"Tempting." She smiles as she taps her finger over her lips, but I can tell by the shifty way she's acting that it isn't going to happen.

"We can nap," I offer.

"And you won't try anything when we lie down in the bed?"

Finally having backed up enough, I have her caged to the countertop with my hips. The steel rod in my sweats answers for me.

"I don't think it'll work."

"Only one way to find out."

"We should nap on the couch."

"We aren't napping." I fling her over my shoulder, delighted in her squeal. Thankfully, Rick doesn't come out of his room this time as I carry her down the hall.

Come to find out it takes orgasms *and* a nap to get her fully relaxed.

Chapter 30

Sophia

"You promised you were relaxed."

I refuse to look over at Colton on the drive to his parents' house.

"I was," I hiss, my fingers tangling in my lap. "I look ridiculous."

Thankfully, Rick decided to drive himself earlier so he's not a witness to me freaking out.

"You're adorable."

"I shouldn't be adorable. You're like twenty years older than me. I should look refined."

"Baby, I don't want you to ever look refined, and there's less than thirteen years between us."

I can't even bask in the sentiment of his words because I'm sitting in the passenger seat of the truck wearing a pair of Rick's athletic leggings and a baggy t-shirt.

"Just swing by my house."

"We're already late."

"That's your fault."

He chuckles. "You're the greedy one."

"I didn't know I had to choose."

The fact is I was exhausted after the orgasms and the nap was a necessity. What I didn't think to do was set an alarm giving me enough time to get home and get changed.

"I smell like you," I hiss, lifting the shirt to my nose. "Your mom is going to know what we've been doing."

"You're an adult."

"Doesn't make it any less embarrassing. Is she going to question why I'm wearing Rick's clothes or why my skin smells like you?" I swivel my head in his direction, and I don't think the vibrant smile on his face has waned in hours.

"My parents know I have sex, Sophia."

I wish I could say the same thing. "Mine don't."

The truck jerks, his foot sliding off the gas and hitting the brakes.

"Yeah, I mean go ahead and live it up. It's a big joke that I'm going to dinner with your parents mere hours after screaming your name while coming on your face. At least they know you have sex, seeing as you have a son and all." My smile turns teasing to something akin to devilry. "My dad probably still thinks I'm a virgin, but don't worry, I'll make sure you're nice and relaxed before we sit down to a meal with him."

He doesn't find my wink comical.

"Wait," he says as I reach for the door handle when he pulls up outside of a lovely one-story home with light blue shutters, and flower boxes on the windows.

"What are you saying?"

"You'll be the first guy I bring home." Maybe my shrug is a little dismissive of the situation, but this man normally has nerves of steel. Is he anxious about meeting my father as more than my internship training officer?

Instead of looking at me, his eyes settle on Rick's truck parked in front of the house.

"They're going to get suspicious if we just keep sitting out here."

"You weren't a virgin."

"Neither were you."

"Your dad didn't meet the man you gave that to?"

I cringe. "Yeah, that's a no. I barely knew him. No way I'd bring him home."

"Oh."

Is that disappointment?

"Look, we both have histories, but I'm not going to sit here and let you think I'm some innocent girl without experience. I mean, I don't have twenty years' worth like some people." I side-eye him, hoping he'll take the jab as a joke. "I haven't taken guys home because I haven't ever found a man worth the trouble until you."

"Trouble?"

"Do you really think that my dad is just going to smile at you, shake your hand, and welcome you into his home?"

"That's what my parents are going to do for you."

He frowns when the shifting of the front curtains draws both of our attention.

"My dad is different. I think being a father to girls is different. Combine that with twenty years in the Marine Corps and another twenty-plus years working for Cerberus, and he's not the most trusting man, especially when it comes to his girls. Max and Tug still get stared down on occasion by him, and they've vowed to cherish her until the day they die. He did, however, invite you to the graduation party—"

"Because he didn't know I wanted to blow my load on your perfect tits," he mutters.

"Don't bring that up during the first dinner with him, and maybe you'll survive to see another day. But my point is, he respects you. If he didn't, he wouldn't have extended the invitation."

"It wasn't the first time I went to the clubhouse."

"I know." I grin, remembering seeing him there months and months ago. His handsome face and that badge on his hip made me grateful I'd gone against my parents' wishes and started working on a degree in criminal justice because it led to the opportunity to do the internship with him. "I saw your handsome face and tight ass last year while you were working Simone Murphy's case. That's the day I decided I wanted to work at the police department for my internship."

He grins, the thoughts of trouble with my dad falling away. "No kidding?"

"I had fantasies about you long before walking into your office that day."

"You're worried about what my parents will think of your clothes." His fingers brush down my face, folding my bottom lip down in the most seductive way. "How are we going to explain my rock-hard cock?"

"Whatever takes the pressure off of me." I press a quick kiss to his lips and hop out of the truck before he can grab me and demand more of my mouth.

"You're playing with fire," he hisses as he catches up to me at the front of the truck.

In a second flat, my back presses to the grill of his truck, the heat from the engine running combined with the bright May sun nearly enough to make me squirm.

"Am I?" I tease.

His fingers tangle in my hair, hips pressed against mine. Damn, this man makes me forget my head.

"Do I need to turn the hose on you two?"

I freeze, my cheeks heating at the baritone voice coming from the front porch.

"They kept me up all night last night," Rick says from somewhere inside.

My eyes widen as I look up at Colton. "I'm going to kill your son."

"I'll help you hide the body," he mutters, adjusting himself with one hand as much as he can while clasping mine with the other.

Mrs. Matthews chuckles, and his dad winks at me as we walk up.

"Ah, young love. I remember those days." I don't deny her words as I step closer. Her arms are out, and I know I won't be able to get out of a hug. I allow this woman, who has only met me once, to wrap her arms around me, and other than my own parents, it may possibly be the best hug I've ever had.

"I'm so glad you're here," she tells me, turning in my arms and keeping her arm around my waist. "I hope you like chicken fried steak."

"Good to see you, too, Mom," Colton mutters as he walks in behind us.

"She's just giving you a minute to calm yourself, son," I hear his dad say, and my cheeks heat even more.

"You have a lovely home, Mrs. Matthews."

"Sally, please, and it would be lovelier if I could get these young men in my life over to repaint the front porch. I asked ages ago, but I doubt it'll ever get done."

"You asked last week, Mom, and the paint you insisted I get is on backorder. Don't try to make me sound like a jerk in front of my girlfriend."

I bite the inside of my lip to keep from reacting. I want to laugh at the easy banter between him and his parents. Even Rick seems comfortable enough to joke around with them. I also want to squeal and jump into his arms for calling me his girlfriend in front of them.

"I'll let it slide this time," Sally says as she directs me to take a seat in the living room. "So, it's official?"

"Official?" Colton asks confused. Bless his nearly geriatric heart.

"They haven't posted it on Facebook or anything yet," Rick mutters.

"I don't have Facebook." Colton looks at me. "Do you?"

"Are you telling me you don't know?" I tease back.

If he's wanted me as long as he claims, then I know he's looked, probably more than once just to be sure.

"We don't have Facebook," Colton confirms. "But yes, we're together."

His mother releases the squeal I was able to hold on to.

"They kept me up—"

"You'll clean the gutters," Colton threatens, and comically Rick slams his mouth shut, winking at me much the same teasingly way his grandad did on my walk of shame up the sidewalk.

"No social media?" Sally asks, and I shake my head. "At all? Even I like to get lost in a little *Tik Tok* every now and then."

"You mean you like to watch half-naked men swing their junk around in gray sweats," Mr. Matthews corrects.

Sally waves her hand dismissively at her husband as Rick scrunches his nose as he pulls out his phone.

"What are you doing?" Colton asks, making me wonder if they have a no-electronics rule on Sundays. This is just another question I need to ask. Honestly, I need to start writing them down because I get distracted while we're alone and they're really starting to pile up.

"Making my accounts private."

"If you're making obscene—"

"Dad," Rick groans. "I'm not. Stop."

Both of the grandparents laugh, and I feel bad for the kid with all the adults in his life picking on him, but then I remember the stunt he pulled with the omelets at breakfast and I realize very quickly he came by it naturally.

My fear of being around his family fades quickly.

"Not even Instagram?" Sally asks, still fixated that I'm a woman in my twenties and not spending hours a day on social media platforms.

"Nope. According to my dad, they're one of the easiest ways to hack your information. It's hard to keep secrets when you practically sign your life away through a company's terms of service without even reading them."

Rick drops his phone in disgust causing everyone in the room to laugh.

"Got something to hide, Ricky?"

Rick isn't laughing as he ignore his grandfather's question.

"And you're related to Diego, the man that runs the Cerberus MC?"

"He's my uncle."

"And that makes Dominic—"

"My dad."

I give both of them a weak smile. We didn't talk about much else other than school that first time I met them. It seems they're diving in deeper this time around, and although Colton warned me they would, it doesn't make it any easier to sit here and answer the questions as they're rapid fired at me.

"Incredible men," Mr. Matthews says with a little awe in his voice.

"Incredible women," Sally adds. "Emmalyn and Khloe both took classes with me when I first started teaching at the community college."

"Small world," I manage.

Maybe Landon isn't the only one I have to worry about spilling the beans. I have to be concerned about everyone who knows about me and Colton slipping up and mentioning it to any one of the thirty or so people I know closely linked to the club. We're going to have to make a game plan to talk to my parents quickly because this isn't going to stay off the radar for much longer.

The conversation comes easy, and just as Colton said, his parents really seem to like me, not that I've ever had a problem with people disliking me, but their approval means the world. I couldn't imagine being in a relationship that the people closest to him didn't agree with. It gets us one step closer to fully being together, and as much of a hard time as I give Colton about my dad, I know he'll be okay with us being together. It may not happen instantaneously, but eventually he'll be able to tell how much I love this man, and he'll come around.

Chapter 31

Colton

"Yes, I can," Sophia says, her lips turning down in a frown that makes me want to kiss it away.

She a temptress of the greatest extremes. There haven't been many days I didn't get out of bed ready to head to the station. My job, although heartbreaking at times, serves a purpose. Rick and that purpose is what has driven me for as long as I can remember.

But now there's a naked woman in my bed, tempting me to stay home and make good on the promises we've whispered over and over to each other this weekend.

"You can't," I argue. "You signed the same damn paperwork I did. There's a no fraternization policy in place."

"It's stupid."

"It's supposed to make things safer at work, less drama." I pull an undershirt over my head, loving the way she seems disappointed with each article I cover my body with. "And before you argue about no one knowing, Monahan already suspects something is going on."

"Does he not know about what's going on with the two women in dispatch?"

"I don't know, but you coming to work with me isn't possible, and it's a bad idea even if the policy wasn't in place."

"Have a hard time concentrating?"

"You know I do. I don't know how I got anything done the last couple of months with you around."

Her mouth hangs open, disbelief on her face. "I'm a professional. I think I can go to work with you and keep my hands to myself for a couple hours."

"I can't say the same," I mutter, reaching into the closet for a pair of slacks. This makes her happy, and I love everything about the grin spreading across her face. "I think we'd spend the day either locked away in my office or down some dark alley."

"I can't even tell you the number of times I pictured myself riding you in the car."

"And saying shit like that is why I'm going to be late for work."

I'm hard as stone, but that's not a new thing around her. Leaving for work knowing she's here, naked between my sheets, is what's causing the problem today.

"You can't blame me. I'm not doing anything to keep you here."

She moans a low throaty sound, and my hand freezes on my zipper.

"What are you doing?"

"Nothing." The sheets move the smallest fraction.

"Where are your hands?"

Rolling her lips between her teeth, she shrugs. "Don't mind me."

"Sophia," I warn, gripping the edge of the comforter and tugging on it slowly.

I'm in complete awe of her gorgeous body, of every sexy inch that's revealed. She doesn't stop what she's doing, the sheet finally pulling away to expose her fingers working over her delicate flesh.

"It feels so good," she whispers.

"Yeah?"

She nods. "Do you like what you see?"

"Fucking love it." My mouth is dry, and I can think of one way to moisten my lips, but getting an inch closer to her would mean explaining my tardiness to my superiors. "Dip them inside."

She does, and the slickness of her arousal makes me ache.

"Jesus, that's perfect. So pink."

"Swollen. I'm so tight, so sensitive from the last couple of days."

"Sore?"

"Tender in the most delicious way."

I lick at my dry lips, reaching into my boxers and stroking my cock. I may not have time to taste her or slide my cock inside of her, but I won't get a damn thing done if I don't take care of myself.

"Let me see," she begs.

The pleading tone of her voice makes my balls tighten, the threat of release imminent. I pull my cock out, my hand working the length of it with expert strokes.

"Small, soft circles," I whisper. "Imagine it's my tongue. God, I love seeing you like this."

She whimpers, obeying my words even though I know she wants to be rougher. My girl likes it hard and fast, and most days that would work for me too, but this morning I want her to burn with the same desperation I'm going to feel the entire time we're apart today.

"Are you close?" Her eyes focus on my working hand. She doesn't answer, but I've become an expert on reading her body these last couple of days. Her stomach muscles flutter, breasts tipped with hard points, and her breath is coming out in short, labored bursts. "I'm going to come so fucking hard."

And it's true, but I'm waiting for her, needing her to tip over the edge before I allow the same relief for myself.

"Colton," she sighs, and I'm fucking done.

Her fingers move faster, her thighs tensing as her eyes flutter closed.

"Watch," I hiss as I take a few steps closer to the bed.

I paint stripes of cum over her bare stomach, groaning with soul-deep pleasure at the way I mark her skin.

Her teeth dig into her lower lip as she pulls her trembling fingers from her pussy, swirling the glistening tips in the mess I made of her.

"Put them in your mou—"

I don't even have to utter the words because her hand is already moving, eyes lighting up with mischievousness as she licks us both away.

"This is going to be the longest day of my life," I complain as I tuck myself away, my hand finally managing to get the zipper all the way up this time. I already know the hours between now and getting back to her are going to drag.

"Are you going to kiss me goodbye?" Her still sleepy face looks up at me.

I couldn't walk away from her right now if I had a gun pointed at my head, so I bend at the waist, groaning at the taste of us on her tongue. It seems filthy and scandalous, but somehow perfect all at the same time. Is this what perfection looks like?

Like I haven't been laid in years, my cock threatens to harden with a jerk.

I cup her cheek, locking my eyes with her when I pull back a few inches.

"I love you."

"I love you, too." The four words aren't just a confession. They sound like a promise, and that's what I'll take when I leave. That's what will make me hold steady throughout the day.

"I won't linger too long, but I'm going to get a shower before I leave."

"I want you here."

"I'll be here when you get back, but I have to go home and get clothes. Maybe pack a bag if you want me to stay over again."

Would it be too soon to tell her I never want her to leave, that lying in this bed even one night alone would be a nightmare?

"I want you here. I want your clothes in the closet, your soaps and bodywash cluttering the bathroom. I want you marking my space and making it your own."

She angles her head to take my lips again.

"We need to talk about how we're going to tell my dad. A couple of nights away from home is one thing, but practically moving in without speaking to him wouldn't end well."

My parents know about us and telling them was no big deal to me, so I don't really understand why my heart kicks so hard at thoughts of telling her dad.

"We have a lot to talk about," I confirm. "This evening?"

She nods. "I'll be here when you get off work."

"There's a spare key hanging on the rack in the kitchen. Rick probably won't get home until after me. He hangs out with friends right after school."

"I'll make sure I'm fully clothed just in case."

I want to ease her mind about my son, but since he hasn't opened up to me about what's going on in his life, it feels like a violation to speak about those things with others.

With one more press of my mouth to hers, I say my goodbyes, my legs heavy as I leave her in my bed.

I make it out the front door and into my truck by sheer will alone, keeping my eyes out the front windshield instead of glancing back at my home.

I'm only going to work, but it's getting back to that part of my life without her that's a struggle. Not to mention the strange feeling I have in my gut that things are going to change soon. Realistically I know they will, but the acid burning deep inside of me feels like a warning that those changes may not be for the best.

I'm not able to hyperfocus on conversations we'll have this evening because I get called out mere minutes after settling behind my desk to check emails.

After clearing the scene—another overdose—I'm able to fire off a few texts to Sophia. It doesn't take long for things to turn sexual, and I'm praying as I look down at a picture of her naked breasts that this never changes. I hope we're just as hot for each other in ten years as we are now.

I explain I have to work and she's making that nearly impossible with images of her perfect tits on my phone, but that doesn't stop the disappointment I feel when she stops texting back.

Chapter 32

Sophia

Being alone in his house should be weird. Nothing is familiar except the scent of our skin on his sheets, but I find that I'm comfortable here. It's not like visiting a distant relative and worrying about being caught looking too long at something that doesn't belong to me.

I don't worry about getting in trouble for picking up and inspecting the framed pictures on the mantel, but I do make a mental note to get more of Rick and Colton together. Like I imagine any busy, single father would, the pictures are more plentiful when Rick was younger, tapering down as he got older. They need more physical proof of their lives, and that's one thing I know I can help with.

I grin at the most recent picture, one of Sally and Franklin with Colton and Rick. Rick doesn't look pleased to be in what can only be described as an ugly Christmas sweater, but what makes it hilarious is the fact that they're all wearing the same one, the only difference being the bow on Sally's wool reindeer head.

What makes it perfect is that we have a picture almost identical to this at my house, only it's my dad with discomfort-filled eyes. As a career Marine in matching footie pajamas, I think he was a very good sport, but there's seldom a time when he tells Mom no if she has an idea.

I could walk around this house all day long and learn a million things about the men that live here, but I also have a ton of things to get done if I want to be back by the time Colton gets off work. I don't want to miss a single second with him.

I can't fully regret the nap I took after my shower because the bed was too inviting to pass up. Colton didn't seem disappointed with the pictures I sent to him either. My dad would lock me away if he found out I sent digital images. I know Colton wouldn't share them, but there's always the risk of someone else getting their hands on his phone.

My nipples bead against the soft t-shirt I'm wearing, reminding me that I still need to get clothes from home as well as check on Izzy. Her entire world has been turned upside down, and I know she was still working out a way to tell her dad about the baby when her truth was spilled long before she was ready.

Keeping on the t-shirt and sweats I took from Colton's drawer, I slide my feet back into my sandals. I start a running list in my mind for all the things I need to grab. Colton may regret offering up closet space after I return. If this is where we both want me to be, then I'm going to need some comforts from home. I grin as I grab the spare key from the kitchen and swirl it on to my own key chain. I wonder how he's going to feel about my fluffy robe and the worn slippers I like to wear on the weekends. I add long pajamas to my list, remembering that there's someone else in this house besides my guy.

I'm light on my feet, filled with utter happiness when I open the front door, only to have that elation blasted away when a masked man grips my face in a gloved hand and shoves me back inside.

I falter. Even after all the training and conversations I had growing up about what to do, my mind can't decide whether to run or stay and fight. Either option seems viable, so why do I just stumble back in shock, as if the masked man will lift the bottom of the mask and reveal himself as Colton.

I know it isn't him in the split second my brain tries to catch up to the situation. He doesn't smell the same. This man's build is smaller in size and rounder in the middle.

I can evaluate all of that, but as I fall on my ass in the entryway, crying out from the pain the impact causes in my tailbone, I still haven't figured out what to do next.

"Please don't hurt me."

I scurry back, my fingers not keeping up with my legs, which makes me land flat on my back, head bouncing off the hard wood under me.

Oh Jesus. Being on the ground is the worst position to be in. He's not as big as Colton, but he's still bigger than me, and basic physics say that he can overpower me easily.

He's going to rape me. It's the very first thought that hits me in the chest as he slams the front door closed and stands over me. The sound echoes around me making me realize I lost the opportunity to scream for help. I attempt to anyway, throwing my head back and yelling at the top of my lungs.

It doesn't take long for him to swing out, clocking me in the cheek to shut me up. Fire burns my face with the hit, my hands instinctively reaching up to cover the wound.

"Shut the fuck up, bitch," he seethes, spittle falling from his lips onto my face.

I kick and scream, bite and claw at him when he picks me up off the ground with a tight grip on my shoulders, and I want to berate myself for worrying about the bruises he's going to leave behind when I know things are probably going to get much, much worse.

I'm thrashing in his arms, unable to hear his threats as he drags me into the kitchen. I try to stomp his foot and get my leg high enough to kick him the balls. I know there's a good chance I'm going to die today, many home invasions end exactly like that, but being raped and then dying seems like too much to go through. If I can hurt that part of him, maybe the death will be quick. At this point, it's the best I can hope for.

It's mid-afternoon, and Colton won't be home for hours. According to him, Rick won't be home until even later, and I see that as a blessing, praying that Colton comes home before his son. I don't want Rick walking in to discover what this man has done to me. No child should have to live with those images in their head.

Tears leak down my cheeks as I'm thrown into a dining room chair with little care.

"Enough," he hisses, producing a length of rope from his pocket. "Keep that shit up and I'll slit your fucking throat."

The threat is enough to make me freeze, even though I know the outcome will still be dire. Maybe talking some sense into him will help, although deep down I know this man came here on a mission, and trying to reason with someone who is brave enough to break into a detective's house isn't going to work.

"This is a cop's house," I say, hoping that maybe it was chosen at random and the threat of extra vigilance at catching him will be enough to get him to leave.

"I fucking know that." My skin burns under the rope as he ties my hands behind the chair. "Detective Colton Matthews is the whole reason I'm here."

"Kincaid is my uncle."

His eyes find mine, a knowing look in the bloodshot depths.

"That so?"

I nod, allowing myself hope that the threat of my family will be enough to make him walk right back out of here.

"I bet they'd be willing to do just about anything to see you safely out of this?"

I swallow, my mouth going so dry, my lips begin to ache.

"Wh-What do you want from Colton?"

"I ask the fucking questions." He hits me again right over the same spot the first blow landed, and it makes my vision go blurry.

I want to sob. I want to hang my head and beg for my life. I want Colton to have never left for work because I know without a doubt that I wouldn't be sitting here in pain. He'd keep me safe. He'd give his own life to protect mine.

And that makes me pause because he has a son. Rick needs his father. Surviving without me is possible, losing that kid isn't.

My spine stiffens, resolve making me as brave as possible in this situation.

"When does he get off work?"

I keep my mouth closed.

"How many guns does he have in the house?"

I still refuse to answer him, squeezing my eyes closed and flinching when he lifts his hand to hit me again. The blow doesn't come, and when I open my eyes, I see him pacing back and forth in the entryway, hands tugging at the top of the ski mask like he wants to pull it off.

He mumbles to himself, but his words are too low for me to understand. I would bet money that this man is either mentally unstable—I mean you kind of have to be to break into someone's house—or he's on drugs.

The latter is confirmed when he pulls a baggie from his pocket before bending over the dining room table. With a dirty card he pulls from his wallet, the man cuts lines of what looks like cocaine before snorting them one after the other.

Now, I don't have any experience with drugs, but four lines in less than a minute seems a little extreme. Is he revving himself up to hurt me more? Is he trying to distance himself from the acts he's about to commit?

As he pours more powder on the table, my entire body begins to tremble uncontrollably. The best outcome would be that he overdoses before Colton gets home. I could handle looking at him seizing on the floor and foaming out of his mouth. The compassion and circumstances Colton reminded me to always be cognizant of while working a case are nowhere to be found in my current situation. I don't care what this man has been through. I don't care who hurt him or what injustices he thinks he's owed retribution for. I know he's here because of a case Colton worked. That was clear when he admitted to knowing whose house this was with Colton's full name and position with the police department.

It's retaliation, and I'm caught right in the damn middle. If I do survive this, I can't see this being a winning point to get my parents over to the side of accepting that we're together.

After he's done snorting the powder, he pulls a disgusting bandana from his pocket, wrapping it around my face and forcing my mouth to open up around it before he ties it at the base of my skull. I fight him as much as I can, but the combativeness is futile. The fabric is tight inside my mouth making my jaw ache almost instantly.

The drugs only make the man pace faster, his movements jerky as frustrated hands swing around.

I'm trying to convince myself that things could be a lot worse when the front doorknob turns. The masked man produces a gun I didn't know he had and points it in that direction.

My heart sinks when Rick and Landon step into the house. Terror fills their eyes, but neither turns to run. A look of defiance crosses Landon's young face when he spots me tied up across the room, and I just know that it's going to be that stubbornness that's going to get him hurt.

Chapter 33

Colton

Today has been the longest day in history. Three calls, endless paperwork, and more than one patrol officer asking about Sophia kept my body busy, but my mind has managed to stay at home with her.

My cock is rock hard with anticipation from her texts, my fingers twitching to smack her perfect little ass for not responding to my last four texts as I pull into the driveway.

She didn't message back when I let her know I was going to be later than I'd originally promised before leaving this morning, and I'm nearly certain the burgers I picked up for us on the way home will get cold on the counter while I spend an hour or so showing her just how much I missed her.

My hand lingers on the door handle inside my truck when I look at the front of my house. It's dark outside already, and my front porch light isn't on. There's no warm glow making the front of my home inviting, and the sight of darkness at my door makes my pulse ramp up. The light is always on. I never wanted Rick to come home to darkness, plus it's a safety feature. As a cop, I also know the porch light is often dismantled by criminals. Common courtesy makes people open their front door when someone knocks, and that invitation into a home goes up when the person inside can't see who is ringing the doorbell, despite knowing it could end badly.

Fear begins to swallow all reasoning as I climb out of the truck, making sure to close the door without making a sound. I feel like a fool as I creep along the side of my house but instinct tells me something is off. Sophia's car is in the driveway, and Rick's is right behind it, which forced me to park a ways up the street.

I hope to look inside and get a good laugh. Maybe the bulb I installed a few months ago was bad, and it burned out too fast. Crazier things have happened.

But I can't take that chance. Dread washes over me when I peek through the curtains outside of the dining room. Sophia, tied to a chair and gagged, has fat tears rolling down bruised cheeks as her eyes dart across the room. Someone has hurt her. I left her here in my home where I thought she was safe, and she's been hurt. Anger laced with fear makes me sweep my eyes down her body. She's clothed, but there's no telling what hell she's been put through or how long she's been at the mercy of those wanting to cause her harm.

My world implodes even more when I see that Rick and Landon are also tied side by side on the floor near her feet. All eyes are across the room, but I can't see who the perpetrator is.

I'm unable to categorize the violation I feel knowing that someone is in my house hurting the people I love most in this world. My hands itch to pull my gun from the holster and blow the motherfucker away, but instinct keeps me moving to get more information. I need to know who is inside and how many people there could possibly be.

Because I'm obsessed with safety and privacy, there isn't another window in the house that leads to more information. Every curtain is pulled tightly closed, and even though I can see one shadow pacing back and forth, I can't be certain that there aren't others inside. I'm forced to head back to my truck, my hands trembling with helplessness as I reach for my phone.

I immediately turn the thing to vibrate because I don't want a call or text to notify those in the house if I go back to the window.

Before I can pull up Monahan's contact information, the damn thing rings in my hand.

"Hello," I answer with hope. "Dominic?"

"Sophia isn't answering her phone."

All hope that he may know about this situation fades away.

"She's ah—"

"Do you know where she is?"

I don't have time to work through why he would be calling me to find her. I don't think that Sophia would've had that conversation without me, but it doesn't matter right now.

"She's at my house—"

"That so?"

"Listen, I'm not going into that right now. There's an assailant holding her, my son, and Landon Andrews hostage. Well, fuck. I don't know if it's a hostage situation, but I just got home and all three are tied up."

"Excuse me?"

"I don't know how many or why they're here, but I need help."

I can hear activity on the other end of the line, and after a few muffled words, it sounds like a herd of elephants moving. The thundering sound reignites the hope that had so easily faded away moments ago.

"Can you get a visual on them?"

"I can't see who has her. I can tell at least one guy is inside, but that's it."

"I need fifteen minutes," Dominic says before he grunts out more commands to those around him.

"I don't have fucking fifteen minutes. I can't risk them being hurt."

"My fucking daughter is in that goddamned house. You'll give me fifteen fucking minutes before you go in there half-cocked and getting someone killed."

"Did you miss the part where my son is trapped inside as well?" I seethe. "I would never do anything to put any of them in danger."

"Fifteen minutes," he grunts before the line goes dead.

My fingers move over the screen of my phone, and thankfully Monahan answers on the first ring. He listens to all the information I have with a calmness I wish I could possess before telling me he's going to get SWAT here as soon as he can. He gives me the same instruction to stand down that Dominic did, and it makes me want to spit fire.

Although I've had training, we haven't had many hostage situations in my time with the police department. Most situations even close to this, the victims are already dead, and we're tasked with getting the perp out alive. Nine times out of ten they either end with suicide or forcing an officer's hand to shoot them.

Knowing the statistics makes it even harder to stand in the street doing nothing.

Dominic somehow manages to make it with his team in ten minutes, and I'm in awe of them as they walk up stealthily in full combat gear. At the police department, we move as quickly as possible but it's clear they're an efficient group.

I don't question the tactical weapons strapped to their chests, but I want to curl in on myself with the way Dominic is looking at me. I've only seen the man a couple of times in person, but it doesn't take an expert to recognize the disappointment in his eyes.

"Only one?" Dominic asks as he steps in beside me, his eyes darting to the house like he can't stand the sight of me.

"That I could see."

Dominic makes a quick hand gesture and a bearded man darts off toward the house. I want to yell, to make the man stop in his tracks. I can't stand and watch as someone else takes a risk that will make my world crumble around me, but the man beside me clamps a hand on my shoulder before I can move.

"There isn't a better sharpshooter within a thousand miles. Let Shadow work."

I feel impotent, utterly helpless as we wait, but long minutes go by without a sound. There's no gunshot. There's no screaming coming from inside. Only the sound of the wind blowing through nearby trees and an occasional dog bark interrupts the atmosphere around us.

"Were there injuries? Could you see all of them?"

I turn to look at Dustin "Kid" Andrews, and although I know he's feeling the same riot of emotions threatening to drag me to my knees on the asphalt, he seems put together and confident in his buddy's ability to save those inside. I wish I shared his certainty.

"I could see Sophia and the boys. They're tied up. She's gagged. She's got bruises on her face like she's been hit, but I didn't see any of that on the boys." I keep my eyes on Dustin instead of turning my attention to Dominic when I continue, "She's been there since I left this morning. The boys wouldn't have gotten there until after school got out. I don't know if they came straight here."

"They did," Dustin confirms, and I focus on his news rather than the growl that emits from deep in Dominic's chest. "I tracked Landon here just before four."

It doesn't surprise me that he would keep that close of tabs on his kid, but knowing Sophia could've been in this house alone with him for hours makes my gut turn sour.

"She texted me just after one. She hasn't texted me since."

"Did her text seem unusual?"

I look back to Dominic.

"No."

"What was the text?"

I take a step back, wondering if he's willing to wrestle my phone from me. I'm in no position to make my confessions now, and I'd never betray Sophia's trust. She wouldn't want her father digging through our text thread.

"She wasn't upset. There was no hidden message. If I thought for a minute there was danger, I would've been here sooner," I explain, hoping he takes it at face value.

She did stop texting me abruptly, but that was only after I insisted I needed to work without distractions. I'll know better next time. If there is a next time.

"One guy," Shadow says, coming back without me noticing. "He along with all three captives are in the east side of the home. There's enough of a crack in the curtains that I can get a shot."

Why the fuck didn't he do it before coming back? Every second they spend inside increases the chances for any one of them to be hurt.

"Go," I urge with a hiss. "Do it."

"We have to wait—thank fuck. Finally."

We watch as the SWAT team pulls up down the street. Monahan isn't far behind in his personal SUV.

I stand to the side as my Chief discusses the situation with Dominic and his men.

"We can't respond the same way we normally would." I jolt at the sound of Dustin's voice beside me. "It's taking everything I have not to run in there, guns blazing and take that fucker down, but I know this situation will be remedied very quickly. They're all going to be okay."

I open my mouth to ask what level of okay he's talking about because alive and okay are two different things. There's no telling the trauma those three have already endured, and we're all out here standing around and doing nothing.

"My guys are all mic'd up. Shadow can let you know what frequency," Dominic says, standing near Monahan as the department's team waits for instruction.

"We need to open a line of communication. We may be able to settle this without bloodshed if we know what he wants."

"We don't even know who it is," I spit, my legs telling me to take care of this shit myself.

"That's why you need to call. I bet he'll pick up if he sees it's you," Monahan assures me.

"Since they're all in danger because of you," Dominic adds, and I know without a doubt, this man will never be happy with me being with his daughter.

And it may not even matter how he feels. I don't see Sophia walking out of that house and into my arms. She's going to blame me as much as her father is.

Chapter 34

Sophia

"Your family?" the guy spits into my phone. "I don't give a shit about your fucking family!"

It's been ringing and beeping with texts for hours, but he didn't answer it until now. He ran out of drugs over thirty minutes ago, and his level of agitation has tripled. Thankfully, he hasn't hit me again, but he was rough when tying up the guys.

I want to reassure them they'll be okay, but I can't muster enough energy for the lie. The gag in my mouth prevents me from speaking, so I opt to look at them, hoping my eyes tell them not to worry.

I watch as a tear rolls down Landon's cheek, the gag in his mouth catching the liquid. Rick leans in closer to him, resting his head on his shoulder, and even though we're living through hell right now, I can appreciate the closeness they share. I look away, not wanting to violate their moment, but the only other thing to look at is the angry man who's yelling into my phone.

He's either talking to Colton or my dad. Either would be a mistake to piss off, but knowing that someone knows that we're in here brings a sense of relief, although I can't help but wonder if it's a false security. Either man would gladly die to make sure we're safe. I pray that whoever it is keeps a calm head on their shoulders.

With frustrated hands, the man finally rips the ski mask off of his head, and it only makes me tremble even more. Not only is he showing his face which is a clear sign he knows he's not going to get away with what he's doing, but I recognize him.

Dennis Milton, the man who killed his girlfriend because she tried to kick him out of their house after she caught him cheating is the man pacing in front of me. How is he out of jail? Colton got a confession from him weeks ago. His case is open and shut. Murderers don't get to post bond, do they? And even if they had the chance, it should've been set so high, he'd never have the ability to afford walking out of jail while he waits for court.

"I already fucking told you what I want!" Milton pulls the phone from his mouth, shouting down at him with malice. "I want my brother out of jail!"

His brother?

Only now do I begin to see the differences. The man in front of us has lighter colored hair and a small scar near his lip that Dennis Milton didn't have during his arrest and interrogation. They're twins if I had to guess.

"Don't talk to me about impossibilities. Just bring him here!"

The pacing continues, his free hand opening and closing repeatedly. I don't know why he chose now to answer the phone, but I can sense that things are going to come to a head very quickly.

I was never called out with Colton to a hostage situation, so I have no clue what the protocol is. I do know that after looking out the window a few minutes ago, that he closed the curtain up tighter than it was prior. I know that he's purposely walking behind us instead of between us and the street.

All of this is concerning, but I also know that Colton wouldn't hide this situation from the police department or my dad. If we have any luck at all, both groups are outside working out a way to put an end to this situation.

I nudge Landon with my foot, angling my head back. He reads it like I knew he would scooting closer to me and keying Rick in on doing it too. We shift closer together, making a smaller target, or if things go down like I think they will, we're a small obstruction to whomever may need to take down Milton.

"Because I want to fucking kill him!" the guy roars into the phone. "He killed Penny. I can't let him get away with it."

He listens, his face sweaty from all the walking around and no doubt the drugs, shaking his head to whatever is being said on the other end of the line.

"No. I have no interest in that fucking kind of justice. I'll take care of it myself. Bring him here. I'll save the taxpayers a ton of fucking money."

He stiffens, his eyes sweeping over the three of us.

"You're not in any place to threaten me, motherfucker. If I don't get what I want, you won't see them alive again."

Both boys are trembling against my own shaking legs. He's made numerous threats since he arrived, but they were mostly random mumbled thoughts. We have all of his attention right now, and the anger in his eyes tells me he has a point to prove and things are going to end badly.

"I loved her. I took a step back. She wanted Dennis. No one ever wants me, but I loved her enough that I wanted to see her happy." A tear rolls down his cheek.

The sight of it makes me whimper. He's beginning to break and not in a good way. He no longer feels any hope.

"He took the most beautiful thing in the world away from me, and if you don't give me what I want, I'm going to do the same to you."

He doesn't even bother hanging up before throwing the phone against the wall where it shatters into a dozen pieces. He's effectively broken any further line of communication.

I want to close my eyes to what I know is coming. The police rarely give in to demands, and if they do, it's only because it somehow gives them the upper hand. Regardless of who is in this house, the Farmington Police would never, and I mean never, let a murderer out of jail so his brother could kill him. It doesn't work that way. I know this, and telling by the shaking going on near my legs, the guys know this too. Milton must be too high from hours of snorting drugs to realize the truth of the situation. Hopefully he keeps believing they'll give in so it gives the police and possibly my dad the chance to rectify this situation before it goes to shit.

"He loves you." He's looking at me with irritation. "And a man who loves a woman that much will do anything to protect her. Do you love him?"

I don't know if he's referring to Colton or my dad, but the answer is still the same.

I nod my head trying to speak and tell him that I do love him, but the gag only allows for muffled sounds.

"A man with both his woman and his son threatened is more likely to get shit done."

Ah, so it was Colton on the phone.

He sniffs, the back of his hand swiping at his running nose.

I can't recall how long it takes an addict to come down and need another fix, but I hope the guys act fast because even though this man has been doing enough drugs to keep a small city high for days, I don't think he's going to keep it together much longer.

"Do you know how hard it's been to look at myself in the mirror?"

I don't bother attempting to answer him as he walks to the mirror hanging on the far wall. Despite his words, he stares at his reflection as if he'll be able to get all of his answers from the man staring back.

"I have his face. I've always been nicer. I'd never hit a woman the way he hit Penny."

He must have memory failure because my face still throbs from his repeated blows.

"Yet, she chose him. They always choose him." He spins to face me. "What is it about abusive men that makes women keep crawling back? Do you like it when men talk down to you? Do you think you can change them?"

I shake my head as he steps closer, hating the way Landon and Rick attempt to stay in front of me. I don't want them to protect me. I need to be the one protecting them.

"Answer me!" he roars.

But how can I? I don't understand women like that because I've never been in that situation, and explaining the psychology of women who stay in abusive relationships would not only be lost on his drug-addled mind, but it's impossible to do so with a fucking gag in my mouth.

I whimper, turning my head to the side when he lifts his hand once again, only this time it isn't his fist he's threatening me with. The gun in his hand is unsteady, but he's close enough to hit his mark without much effort.

I plead with my eyes, but it's clear he's no longer seeing me. I'm not Sophia, Colton's girlfriend. I'm Penny, the woman who broke his heart by making the wrong choice in brothers.

"You didn't have to die. We would've been so happy together." His words come out broken and filled with palpable pain, but I have no doubt Penny's life would've been ruined with either one of them. She may not have been hit, although his actions tonight make me doubt that, but being in a relationship with an addict brings its own set of problems.

"Don't worry," he whispers, lowering the gun and cupping the side of my face with his free hand. "When the night is over, we'll finally be together."

Chapter 35

Colton

I feel like I've been struck with an invisible blow when the call ends. I tried to keep my cool, but the man is threatening my entire fucking world. Losing either of them would destroy me. Losing both of them is a tragedy I'll never come back from.

For some reason, it's in this moment that the many conversations I've had with Sophia while working come back to me. I told her compassion is fleeting. I explained that people are put in impossible situations. Sometimes, it's because of a mental break. At other times, it's because they've been struck so hard by loss that they see no other way out. It seldomly entails actual psycho or sociopathic reasons. There are mitigating circumstances that put Sophia and Rick in this man's path tonight, but I can't muster an ounce of that compassion. I can't see being satisfied with any other outcome than this man being carried away from here in a fucking body bag.

"He closed the curtain," Shadow says, his voice coming over the mic. "I no longer have a shot. Get with Max and tell him to get us ears inside."

It's mere minutes before the conversation inside is transmitting. Max, a guy I'm guessing that works for Cerberus, was able to tap into Landon's phone. The muffled words are hard to hear because the phone is in his pocket, but the dangerousness of the situation comes across loud and clear.

"He's insane," Monahan says after hearing the way he's talking to Sophia. "Like clinically. Did you know about the link between him and Penny?"

"We knew he had a twin. That came out in the investigation. Both brothers have spent a little time in jail. Roger, the man inside, has a few possession charges. He was picked up for a drunk and disorderly a couple months ago, but we didn't dig enough into his life to find out he was in love with his brother's girl," I explain.

"Probably not something he talked to anyone about," Dominic says, giving me a small concession.

"Obviously, we can't give him what he wants," Monahan says out loud even though we all know it.

Unintelligible garbles come through the tap in Landon's phone followed by sobs. Dominic is slowly losing his cool. The ice-man stature he arrived with has been slowly melting away, and now I can see he's just as worried as I've felt since I pulled up and noticed the front porch light out.

"I love her. My son is inside. Another young man I'm responsible for is sitting beside the both of them," I tell anyone standing close enough to hear. "We have to fucking do something. He's devolving and shit is going to go down sooner rather than later."

Dominic's jaw twitches at my confession, but he refuses to look in my direction. It's clear he blames me. Hell, I blame me. If it weren't for my involvement in the case, this wouldn't be happening. No matter how much the reasonable part of my brain tries to tell me that this situation could happen at any point to any officer over the course of their career, this isn't happening years ago to someone else. It's happening to me.

I'm to blame.

"Peterson is an excellent shot. If we can get him in the hous—"

"Shadow is better," Dominic interrupts. "Let my guys handle this, Chief."

Monahan shakes his head. "This is Farmington jurisdiction."

"You're going to let that come into play here?" Dominic hisses, and I bet he's seconds away from wrapping his hands around my boss's throat. "We don't have time to spend measuring our dicks out here. Shadow has decades of experience. He's not some cowboy wanting a little piece of the glory. Sophia and Landon are just as much family to him as they are to us, and even if they weren't, he'd protect all three of them with his own life. That's an oath he took."

"My guy took an oath, too, and he's not a fucking cowboy looking for glory," Monahan argues.

"When was the last time he had to pull his gun or the trigger on a man in his scope? When was the last time he had to sneak into a building and take out a suspect? This month? This year? At any point in his career?" Dominic points in the direction of the house, and I know he's indicating Shadow who's been out of sight for a while. "Shadow did that shit three weeks ago. I'm not saying your guy is bad. I'm saying my guy is better."

Dominic has a point, and although I don't know Shadow, my confidence in his abilities grows with each word that comes out of his mouth.

"He can get in there and take that fucker out without the mice in the wall knowing he's in there," Dominic continues. "We can end this shit in seconds."

I don't have mice, but I understand the sentiment.

Monahan looks from Dominic to the SWAT team waiting on his orders. Peterson is the one to finally step forward, the heaviness of his gear a different sight than when he's on normal patrol.

"He's got a point. I'm not a coward, and I'm confident in my skills, but my training is no fucking match for that other guy's experience. It doesn't even compare."

Dominic nods at him, knowing it takes a real man to step up and say that, especially coming from a cop. We all carry this inflated sense of worth and bravado. Yeah, we scare as easily as the next guy, but it's dangerous to show that in our line of work. Most cops walk around acting like they're bulletproof all the while knowing they'll be the first to take lethal gunfire if shit goes down. It's a very tenuous line to straddle.

"If this goes bad," Monahan mutters, "it's my ass on the line."

"The longer we wait, the higher the chance," Dominic says, his stance as strong as it was when he first arrived.

"Have your guy handle it," Monahan finally concedes, and I know it takes a good man to act with what he knows is best rather than letting protocol control his decisions.

The Farmington SWAT team moves back as Dominic issues commands into the mic. I know they'll step back in if given the command, but they seem okay with letting the Cerberus team take the lead.

"They're going to be fine," Dustin says at my side. "I trust that man with my life."

I nod my head, knowing I have to trust him with mine as well. My arms tremble, muscles needing to do something to burn off the extra energy I can't seem to get rid of, but I stand as stock still as Dominic does. He's got a lot to lose here tonight as well, but I don't think I'll ever be as calm in situations like this.

Maybe it's his years of experience or his assuredness in his guy's skills. Maybe it's a combination of both, but I bet deep in his soul, he's screaming as loud as I am.

The insane man in my house represents everything that's wrong with the world. Turning grief and anger into acts of violence won't solve a damn thing here tonight. Coming here, no doubt prepared to die, from what we heard him saying to Sophia, was his plan all along, and if Shadow doesn't move fast this bad situation is going to quickly turn to tragedy.

"Colton," Dominic hisses, and I snap out of my racing thoughts and look at him. "Best point of entrance?"

"The master bedroom on the west side of the house is furthest from where they are. Less chance of being heard."

He nods at me, relaying that information.

"I hope this was the right fucking choice," Monahan says as he rests a reassuring hand on my shoulder.

I don't know if the touch is meant to calm me or keep me in place so Shadow can get the job done.

"Me too," I whisper. "Me fucking, too."

Chapter 36

Sophia

I don't realize how calming this guy's pacing was until he stops. He looks at his empty wrist as if there would normally be a watch there. People planning to die sometimes take things off and leave them behind, either just to prepare or because they want to leave tokens and sentimental things behind. People planning to jump to their deaths remove their glasses, and it can be argued they do that so they don't see the fall coming or because it's what they do every night before they go to sleep.

The coked-out man on the other side of the room seems resolved, calming completely until he's standing directly in front of me.

"They aren't going to bring Dennis here."

"They will," I argue, even though I know he can't understand my words. "They will."

I can't stop the sobs from escaping, no matter how hard it is to breathe. My throat is dry and agitated from having the gag in my mouth, and I find it strange that's what I choose to focus on seconds before I die.

I scream when splatter hits my face wanting to die quickly knowing he's shot one of the boys first. They didn't deserve this. Neither boy got the chance to live. None of us will. Heaviness weighs me down, and honestly it's a lot more peaceful than I thought it would be.

An odd sense of calm washes over me. I was loved. It may not have been for long, but I was raised by wonderful parents. I have the best sister and friends anyone could ask for, and Colton loved me. I know he did. So I guess technically, I've had it all.

But then realization slaps me in the face. I won't get to walk down the aisle toward the man of my dreams or have a real job. I'll never know what it's like to feel a child move inside of me. There's so much I'm going to miss.

"Soph, open your eyes. Are you okay?"

A swarm of people surround us, but it doesn't stop the screaming when I watch another masked man roll the dead guy off my lap.

"Look at me." I can't. I just can't. "Sophia Anderson, open your eyes."

That voice. I know that voice. It assured me everything would be okay when I had nightmares. That voice chastised me when I got caught swimming in the lake alone when I was five. That voice promised to protect me forever.

"Daddy?" Dark eyes, exactly like mine, are inches from my face, and rough, loving hands cup my cheeks.

I don't know why I called him that. I haven't called him anything other than dad for a long time. Maybe it's the memories flooding me from my childhood or him following through on so many promises.

"It's gonna be okay, baby. Look at me." Tears stain my cheeks, and he wipes them away with a gentle thumb. "Are you hurt anywhere?"

"The boys," I whimper. "The boys."

"They're fine. Look." Dad shifts out of the way so I can see Dustin with his arms wrapped around Landon. Colton is clinging to a sobbing Rick, his eyes focused on me over his shoulder. "Hold tight. It's over. It's over, baby. You're safe."

My dad isn't one to waste words, but it seems the situation calls for it, and I know the repetition is to reassure me. I would gamble that he's in need of reassurance as well. He flips open a knife, making easy work of the ropes holding me in place, but before I can stand, he sweeps me up in his muscled arms and carries me out of the house.

"Dad, put me down. I can walk."

He doesn't listen as his legs carry me away from the house.

"Dad!" I snap. "Put me down."

He freezes, his eyes finding mine, but he doesn't open his mouth to argue as he lowers my feet to the ground.

"I can't leave you here."

"I have to stay."

"There's a dead body in the house, Sophia. Let me take you home where it's safe."

"The guy is dead. I'm no longer in danger."

"You'll always be in danger."

I don't know if he means with Colton or in life in general. Knowing my dad and the caution he raised me with, he means the latter.

"I love him."

Confessions right after a traumatic event when everything is heightened can be taken seriously, right?

His eyes search mine and I don't know if he's trying to determine if I'm speaking the truth or if he's giving me a chance to change my mind.

"Please?" The one word asks a million questions.

Please let me love him.

Please be okay with my choice.

Please don't hate me because of the choices I've made.

Please remember what it was like when you fell in love with Mom.

I don't know how many questions his simple nod answers, but my feet are moving the second he does it.

I don't hesitate running back into the house where the man who terrorized me lies dead on the carpet in a pool of blood. I don't give the police and Cerberus guys milling around a second glance. The moment Colton and Rick are in sight, I rush to them and wrap my arms around them both.

They envelop me in an embrace, both of them clinging to me. I sob from fear and relief, from knowing how close I came to losing this. God, I don't think I'll ever be able to let them go. Warm tears combine with mine, and I look up to see utter devastation written all over Colton's face.

"Shh," I say, pressing a shaking finger to his lips before he can speak.

I know what he's going to say, but warnings against loving him isn't something I can take right now.

"We're fine. We're safe."

"I'm smothered," Rick jokes as he takes a step back, but the evidence of his own fear continues to pour from his eyes.

He notices me looking at him and quickly wipes his eyes.

"I'm going to stay with Landon tonight."

"Like hell—"

"I think that's a great idea. He'll be safe on Cerberus property," Dustin says as he steps up to us, clearing his throat. "I imagine you two are going to need some time alone."

My cheeks flame. Telling your dad you love someone is worlds away from one of the guys on his team, a man that helped raise me, hinting at anything sexual in nature.

"Landon needs me," Rick argues, his eyes now pleading with his dad to understand.

I know Colton has the same suspicions as I do when he gives his son a simple nod. Rick groans when Colton wraps his arms around him one last time, squeezing him to his chest, but as much noise as Rick is making, I don't miss the fact that he holds his dad even tighter.

"Be safe," Colton whispers. "Call me if you need me."

"I will, Dad." Rick walks out of the house with Landon and Dustin.

Colton wraps his arms around me once again, and there's so much emotion between us, it's as if we can both just forget about the dead guy ten feet away and the people walking around.

"We're standing in the middle of an active crime scene," I mutter against his chest, reluctant to ever let go of him again.

"You have to give a statement."

I know I do. I've been on the other side of this situation before, but having lived it makes each one of those scenes I went to with him seem different. Being the victim sucks, and although I know I may never get this night out of my head, I hope I can move past it.

"He's the one that sent that letter."

"A warrant was signed that day, and people have been actively looking for him, but a man who doesn't want to be found can easily avoid detection."

My fears, something I tried to convince myself were an overreaction, are justified.

"Look at me." Colton takes a step back, holding my face in gentle palms as he looks me in the eye. "I took that situation seriously. I did everything I could to track him down and bring him in. I don't want you to think tonight happened because I thought it was no big deal."

"I know." I nod my head, hoping the action combined with my words are enough for him.

As much as Colton complained about being distracted with me around, the man did damn fine police work. Downtime was nearly nonexistent where he was concerned, and I think that was a lot of his appeal. Maybe it's another one of those traits from my dad—that daddy positivity—that made him attractive to me. I know a good man when I see one because I was raised around a dozen of them growing up in Cerberus.

"Can she give her statement in the morning?" Colton asks over my shoulder, and I turn, meeting the eyes of Chief Monahan.

"First thing," Monahan confirms. "So that means you need to pack a bag and get out of here. I'll make sure crime scene cleanup is scheduled for when we're done."

I don't know how but I manage to fall asleep nearly seconds after Colton drives away from his house. I wake as he lifts me out of the seat.

"Where are we?" I whisper against his warm, firm chest.

"Hampton Inn."

A laugh escapes my lips, and I can feel his chest moving up and down with his own silent laughter.

"Talk about full circle."

He presses his lips against the top of my head before releasing me so I can stand.

"I don't want to lose you, but—"

"You won't."

"I'll understand if this was too much for you. Did he hurt you?"

I angle my face to the light. Gentle fingers brush over the tender spots on my face.

"Did he try to—"

"No. Nothing like that. He didn't. I don't think it was ever his intention. Don't even get that mess in your head. I'm fine."

"I can't stop thinking about the way I saw you tied up and in pain."

I press my mouth to his, effectively shutting him up. We have a lot to talk about, but none of those conversations need to happen tonight.

"I love you. Tonight. Tomorrow. In fifty years and every single day in between. That's all that matters right now."

"You're an amazing woman. You know that, right?"

I smile up at him, cherishing the heat of his body and the security of his arms around me.

"You know there's always a chance of getting hurt if you're involved with me."

"Are you going to hurt me?"

"I'd die before that ever happens."

"And that's why you're stuck with me."

It's his turn to lower his mouth to mine, the kissing staying just on this side of public lewdness.

"Take me upstairs so I can sleep in your arms?"

I squeal in delight when he once again sweeps me off my feet. I press my nose to the column of his neck, and will every bad thought from my head. There's no place for any of it while we're holding each other.

Chapter 37

Colton

"Even after everything you've seen and done as a cop, you're still nervous about this?"

I side-eye Sophia, unable to fully appreciate the humor in her tone.

"You put your life in danger every day," she reminds me.

"Are you saying my life is in danger?"

She shrugs, her eyes pointed toward the house. "Not necessarily."

"That isn't a no."

"I mean, he already knows, right? He's had time to work through things."

"He's had less than twelve hours," I remind her.

"He processes things quickly. It's imperative in his line of work."

"How many times is the man going to be told his daughter is in love?"

"Hopefully only twice." She winks at me, her teeth digging into her bottom lip to keep from smiling.

"Twice?" That hits me wrong.

"At least you're only one guy. Jasmine had to have this conversation, and I don't imagine it was easy to tell my dad that she was in love with two guys at the same time. Well, Dad actually walked in on her with both of them, so the conversation went a little differently."

"Jesus, Sophia. Really?"

"No joke. It was the talk of the clubhouse for a while."

"No." I shake my head, hands running over the top of my head. "Are you really talking about your sister's three-way minutes before I have to face your father?"

"Does that turn you on?"

"No," I say truthfully. "I'll never share you. Ever. But that sultry tone in your voice makes me want to choke you with my dick."

"Is that so?" She turns her body toward me, her hand falling to my thigh.

I push it away like it's burning me, and in a way, I guess it is. I think I'll always run hot for this woman, but now is not the time and in her parents' driveway is definitely not the place.

"Is this how the day is going to go?"

She licks her lips. "If you're lucky."

"Not that. Damn it, woman. Can you get control of yourself?"

"I thought you liked me out of control. This morning when I—"

"Stop!" I can't help the laugh that slips out. "You're maddening."

"Is your cock hard."

"You know it is," I grumble. "I don't want to be disrespectful."

"We can do this another time."

"You saw the curtains flutter when we pulled up. They know we're here. I don't want to have to explain leaving."

"I'm sure they saw us on the camera monitors before the curtains fluttered."

My eyes dart around. If there are cameras, they're well-hidden because I don't see them.

"There are cameras?" I shift in my seat, willing my cock to deflate.

"Of course there are cameras."

"Are you purposely trying to psych me up for this?"

She shrugs again. "You think better on your feet when your adrenaline is up."

"I'm nervous," I confess.

"And that isn't going to help."

I follow her eyes, watching with trepidation as an SUV pulls up beside us. Sophia's sister and two men climb out, all three giving us a little wave before going inside the house.

"Great. Now we have an audience."

"You'll be fine, champ." She smacks my chest like a teammate and climbs out.

I manage to catch up with her at the front of the truck, clasping her hand like a lifeline.

Laughter hits me when we step inside the house, but once the front door closes us in, the sound drops away.

Sophia's sister is standing in the center of the living room with a man on either side of her. Her eyes are shining as they dart between Sophia and me, but she doesn't speak. I wouldn't be surprised if there's popcorn in the damn microwave with the way they're all looking at us. It seems we're the entertainment for the day.

"Kingston," one of the guys says as he steps forward with his hand out.

"Max," the other says in introduction, offering his hand as well. "It won't be as bad as you're thinking. I promise."

"Our situation was bad," Kingston adds with a sly grin. "At least you have clothes on."

Both Sophia and Jasmine laugh like it's funny I'm moments away from facing the firing squad.

"Colton," booms from the other side of the room.

"Just don't lie about anything. He'll know," Max hisses before they all make a hasty exit.

"Hey, Dad," my girl says as Dominic crosses the room. He presses his lips to her temple, but his eyes never leave mine. "Go easy on him."

She smacks his chest, much the same like she did mine before climbing out of the truck, then that beautiful traitor walks away.

She. Walks. Away!

She leaves me alone in the room that may soon end up a crime scene.

I swallow, trying to convince myself this is no big deal. We're both adults. We've done nothing wrong. I love her for heaven's sake. All of that should count for something, but what the hell do I know? I don't have a daughter.

"Sir," I say, holding my hand out to him.

He looks down at the offering, his eyes scrunching just a bit in the corners, but he takes my hand, albeit squeezing too hard for comfort.

"Have a seat." He sweeps his hand in the direction of the couch, but even as I lower myself to the sofa, I'm wondering if requesting to stay standing is an option. "You seem nervous."

My eyes dart toward movement, and I see the entire damn family watching from the other room. There isn't popcorn, but Max is eating handfuls of cereal from the box, his eyes glued on us, so it's practically the same thing.

"A little," I admit because I was told not to lie. He's an expert in his field, so there's no doubt he can see the flop of sweat forming on my brow.

"Never sat down and had a conversation with a girl's dad before?"

"No."

"Because you only use women?"

My eyes meet his, anger swimming in my gut. Is that the type of man he thinks I am?

"You have a son."

"And my ex-wife was raised without a father. Her mother wasn't around much either."

"Your parents are still married?"

"Happily."

"Any issue with us meeting them?"

"None."

"Are you going to keep giving me single word answers?"

"If you keep asking single word questions."

His lip twitches, and for the life of me, I can't tell if he thinks it's funny or if he's preparing to attack.

"You love my little girl."

"With all my heart."

"What are your intentions?"

We're really doing this? I thought this only happened in the movies.

I lift my eyes from him, landing on Sophia in the kitchen. She's positively gorgeous, radiant even.

"I'm going to spend the rest of my life making her happy."

"And if she doesn't want that?"

The warning is clear in his voice.

"Then I guess I'll be walking away with a broken heart."

"You'd give up so easily?"

This feels like a trap.

"I would never do what Milton did last night, but I figure if I work hard every day to keep her, she's more likely to stay. She loves me, too, and I cherish that like a gift." I meet his eyes. "If she changes her mind, I'll have to accept that. I may never be whole again, but I also have a son to worry about."

He nods in understanding. "But you haven't had a serious relationship in years."

"I know how to treat a woman right, sir. I was raised by an incredible man and raised in a household full of love. I may be a single father, but Rick was also raised in a household full of love."

"What happens when she leaves for school?"

I swallow, not wanting to think about her being gone, but we discussed this last night.

"I'll wait for her. I spend as much of my free time going to see her. We'll make it work, but she mentioned last night that she wanted to stay in town and complete the degree online."

He sits back on the sofa, crossing his ankle over the opposite knee. I'm not an expert on his emotions, but I think he's happy with this news.

"I'll support whatever decision she makes. I know I've lived a lot of my life already, and she needs the opportunity to do the same."

"And if she gets pregnant?"

This makes me pause, but there's no way to hide the smile. "We're safe."

Did I just admit to sleeping with this man's daughter? I mean, surely he knows it's happened or is going to happen, but confessing it out loud is weird for everyone.

"Safe?"

"I plan to marry her, sir. If she wants babies, I'll give her a dozen."

"Are you asking permission?"

"No."

His eyes narrow again.

"I won't let anyone stand between us. Absolutely no one, and I don't mean that as any form of disrespect. Your blessing would be nice, though. I don't want her thinking she has to choose."

"I would never put her in that position. I want her happy."

I look over his shoulder once again, meeting Sophia's eyes. I want to touch her skin and have her pressed against me. She's only across the room, and I miss her already. Her delicate features soften even further with my eyes on her, and if I wasn't so entranced, I'd find it comical the way Kingston's eyes dart back and forth between us like he's afraid he's going to miss something.

"I'm happy if she's happy."

"I'll spend every second of my life making sure she is."

"I understand the appeal. Makayla is a bit younger than I am, but if you don't stop looking at my daughter like you're undressing her with your eyes, I may have to punch you in the nose."

I wink at Sophia before refocusing on Dominic.

"I also understand what it's like to take on the responsibilities of another kid," he says, leaving that hanging in the air.

"Rick and Sophia get along very well."

"I'm not happy you guys hid what was going on."

"It's very new," I explain. "The attraction was there, but nothing umm... happened until after the graduation party. I didn't abuse my power or use her internship in a negative way. I've loved her long before I—" I have to look away, my hand immediately going to the back of my neck. "The physical relationship hasn't been going on very long. It's new. Very new. Like days. Just a couple days. Day three. This is day three."

Did someone turn up the heat to make me sweat on purpose? Why am I rambling? I feel like a suspect, only it's my own volition that's keeping me here rather than steel cuffs chained to a table.

"Are you done interrogating him?" Relief washes over me as Sophia steps up to us, but then she sits on my lap, wrapping her arms around my shoulders. "Everyone is ready for brunch."

I don't know if I should push her off my lap because Dominic is watching us like he's assessing the situation and taking notes, but on instinct, my arms go around her as well.

Dominic nods once before standing up and heading into the kitchen.

"Jesus," I hiss, keeping my voice as low as I can manage. "That was intense."

"I think you passed the test," she whispers, pressing her lips to my jaw.

We could be in the middle of a battlefield and that one simple action would calm me.

"I was willing to fight him for you." It's mostly the truth. The man is a massive brick wall, and I'm sure even at his age he could kill me with his bare hands. "I would've probably died, but you're worth it."

She chuckles, her nose resting against my neck.

"You may still get your chance. We haven't told him I'm moving in with you yet."

Chapter 38

Sophia
Several Months Later

"It's weird."

I look across the room, unable to deny his words. My parents and his parents are chatting with Uncle Diego and Aunt Emmalyn. They're all smiling and joking with one another.

"It's a little strange," I admit.

"My dad is wearing jeans, Sophia. And a pair of fucking combat boots."

I roll my lips between my teeth to keep from smiling. "Think he'll buy a Harley next?"

"My mom would never allow it."

"I overheard her telling Khloe that she always wanted to feel the wind in her hair."

He snaps his face in my direction. "Seriously? What have we done?"

"Besides falling in love and bringing two families together?"

His gaze focuses on my lips, and a very familiar warmth fills my blood. We're insatiable when we're together, unable to keep our hands to ourselves. It's always our biggest concern when we go out in public. Getting handsy at the clubhouse isn't an option, but it doesn't stop the desire from pooling in my stomach.

"You've got to stop looking at me like that," I warn. "Do you want to end up in the empty bedroom again?"

He nods his head slowly, and the temptation is real.

"Stop." I swat at him, causing him to laugh.

"You guys are disgusting," Izzy groans beside us. "Can't you turn it off even for a few hours?"

I release Colton's hand to turn my attention to my best friend. She shifts her weight on the sofa, grimacing. It's clear she isn't comfortable.

"What's wrong?" I press my hand to her round belly. "Feeling a little left out?"

"How can I feel left out when I'm right in the middle of your foreplay?"

"Maybe you just need to get laid."

Her nose scrunches up, and Colton chuckles. He's long given up telling me to keep my ideas in my head. Training him has been so easy.

"Umm..." She points to her very pregnant belly. "No one wants to touch me."

"You'd be surprised," Jasmine interjects. "There are many men attracted to pregnant women."

"True," Gigi adds. "There are all types of fetishes out there."

Izzy looks around the room, and I know she's checking the location of her dad. He knows she's pregnant and accepted it long ago, but he'll never be a man okay with discussing sex so openly with his daughter. Gigi, her stepmother who is only a few years older than her, has no qualms about it.

"I'm uncomfortable," Apollo says as he stands from the sofa.

"Only because Hound still thinks you're the one that got her pregnant," Max teases.

Apollo's eyes widen as he stares down at Izzy. "I thought you cleared that up."

I grin as he looks down at her belly before walking away.

"He'd definitely scratch that itch for you," I murmur.

"Not ever going to happen," my best friend says, but when her eyes follow him all the way across the room, it makes me wonder if she believes her own words.

"Self-love isn't bad either," Gigi says when the group grows silent.

Leave it to her to say something like that.

"My orgasms are always stronger when I'm pregnant." Gigi presses a soft hand to her tiny bump.

"I'm not discussing this with you," Izzy snaps with mild disgust. She grunts when she tries to stand up, the roundness of her belly making it hard to gain leverage to get off the couch.

Like the good friend I am, I push on her back to help even though I don't want her disappearing right now. We both just started our online programs. She's trying to finish up as many hours as she can before the baby arrives, and I'm in my first semester of graduate school. I spend most of my free time with Colton, and she's been withdrawing more and more.

I make a mental note to spend more time with her.

"Don't go," I whisper, my hand clinging to hers, but all she does is stare down at me like I have two heads.

"I have to pee. Wanna come with me?"

"That's another popular fetish," Gigi offers out of nowhere.

Several people chuckle, making Izzy scrunch her nose again. The woman is becoming an expert on the action.

The front door opens before she can walk away, and of course everyone in the room turns their heads.

Lawson walks in beaming, a wide smile on his handsome face. Behind him is Drew, who has been in lock-up for the last couple of months while waiting for things to play out after his arrest. I haven't had many interactions with the man, but the agitated look on his face as he steps inside is new. From what I remember of him, he was always smiling, always joking. He is the comic relief in contrast to Lawson who tends to be the more serious brother.

"That's Drew," I whisper to Colton who turns his head to look.

We've had many conversations about what happened with him, but I had no clue he'd be coming back here. All of his family, other than Lawson, is in New England.

"Oh," Izzy whispers, and I smile because no matter how sour Drew looks, he's just as good-looking as his older brother.

Maybe her luck is looking up?

Drew's eyes dart around the room, taking in the scene like I would expect any trained cop would do, but then his eyes land on Izzy and he freezes. She shifts on her feet when his eyes sweep down the length of her. Tension fills the room when he stares at her belly.

I expect questions. I expect emotions from both of them.

What I don't expect is for Drew to turn around without a word and walk back out the front door.

THE END
Ready for more Cerberus MC?
Grab Drew: Cerberus MC Book 15 Today!

Social Media Links

FB Author Page
FB Author Group
Twitter
Instagram
BookBub
Newsletter

OTHER BOOKS FROM MARIE JAMES

Newest Series
Blackbridge Security
Hostile Territory
Shot in the Dark
Contingency Plan

Standalones
Crowd Pleaser
Macon
We Said Forever
More Than a Memory

Cole Brothers SERIES
Love Me Like That
Teach Me Like That

Cerberus MC
Kincaid: Cerberus MC Book 1
Kid: Cerberus MC Book 2
Shadow: Cerberus MC Book 3
Dominic: Cerberus MC Book 4
Snatch: Cerberus MC Book 5
Lawson: Cerberus MC Book 6
Hound: Cerberus MC Book 7
Griffin: Cerberus MC Book 8
Samson: Cerberus MC Book 9
Tug: Cerberus MC Book 10
Scooter: Cerberus MC Book 11
Cannon: Cerberus MC Book 12
Rocker: Cerberus MC Book 13
Colton: Cerberus MC Book 14
Cerberus MC Box Set 1
Cerberus MC Box Set 2
Cerberus MC Box Set 3

Ravens Ruin MC
Desperate Beginnings: **Prequel**

Grab it for free HERE**!**

Book 1: Sins of the Father
Book 2: Luck of the Devil
Book 3: Dancing with the Devil

MM Romance
Grinder
Taunting Tony

Westover Prep Series
(bully/enemies to lovers romance)
One-Eighty
Catch Twenty-Two

Made in the USA
Coppell, TX
24 January 2025